AF433170

Frost Place Stories

From Forest Bluff

KJ Lawlor

I dedicate this collection of short stories to my Father, who was also my
best friend.
Joseph Patrick Lawlor Jr. 1925-2012

And to my lovely Wife, Leena Anneli Saarela, for her unselfish and
enduring support in helping me with my endeavours.

Acknowledgements

Thank you to Jean Reynolds, Ph.D. for her exquisite expertise in manuscript quality. Her enthusiasm for literature and writing is contagious. I thank her for encouraging me to forge ahead with my writing.

Thank you to my wife Leena Anneli Saarela, for her unwavering support during good times and bad.

Table of Contents

Accordion Wars

I just couldn't get in to it. The sound of it, the sheet music, the damn song. No matter how hard I practiced, and no matter how much Mrs. Ghianati, my accordion teacher, praised my technique; I hated it! Ok, Burt Bacharach's "Alfie," sounds great on a grand piano, played ever so gently and sung by Dionne Warwick, but Jesus Lord, not on the accordion! Mrs. G didn't see, or hear it that way. She was a good teacher, an expert and aficionado of the accordion; I can't stress this enough! Mrs. G and her husband, Ron, aspired to show that ANY piece of music, can be played and sounds amazing on the accordion. At the age of thirteen, I begged to differ.

I began playing accordion when I was seven. It was by choice. I heard and watched my Aunt Margie play her shiny pearl lacquered accordion at her farm house in Iowa in 1966. I was sold. Something about this instrument mesmerized me. The buttons on the left side and the keyboard on the right. This was not only a fascination with gadgetry but to make music with this wind box was something I had to conquer; if not accordion, then the bagpipes. After coming home from the farm Thanksgiving, the search for an accordion teacher was in order.

Finding an accordion teacher where we lived wasn't easy. My dad was a language teacher, but a musician at heart. He played piano by ear, and always wanted to study music seriously but, did not have the parental support. Money wasn't an issue; society and stigmas were. My dad lived vicariously through my musical instruments. Accordion was the first, and by all measures the most memorable. From the age of seven to thirteen, I was tutored weekly every Saturday morning at 10am sharp. Mrs. G was a stickler for time. She also had a small and cramped home, making students wait outside before and after our lessons. Mind you, this was Northern Illinois and the weather was either miserable or cold and rainy. My dad was my chauffeur, and often late to pick me up, but not to drop me off. I remember sitting on my accordion case in blizzard conditions nodding at the German, Polish and Italian kids from neighboring towns standing at the back door waiting to get the OK to enter the kitchen. Once getting the OK from Mrs. G, the tight entry way was wonderfully warm and smelled of boiling pasta and garlic. It was surreal then and even now that I think about it; the sounds of kids playing "Julida Polka" in the WASPY city limits. Shocking!

The accordion, played well, can do so much to enhance a melody. It possesses a musical cultural history that spans the entire world. Treasured as a sound that evokes an auditory ambiance that is unique to so many nationalities and ethnic celebrations. Even so, the accordion gets a lot of bad press; associated with immigrants, outsiders and blue-collar folks. Frankly, I could have cared less about this sentiment. I wasn't aware of this until later. My dad loved it and so did my immigrant Finnish mother. Even though we lived in a community of Philistines, when I played at parties and family gatherings, I was a hit! Hell, I could burn out a bunch of polkas, Italian and Spanish love songs and even Hava Nagila! I'd have even the predictably snooty enjoying themselves.

Every Spring, Mrs. G would gather her accordion students together to discuss the annual Illinois Music Competitions. We were all required to participate in this state-wide accordion meet. It was a ritual for the Ghianati. I wasn't particularly excited about this event, even though the previous year (1971), I won first place for my performance of "Never on Sunday." Each student was selected to play a solo piece of music, which, up till this year wasn't an issue. But the part I was dreading most was the group ensemble positions. I preferred solo stuff, especially in an accordion competition, nevertheless, was to be. On a select Saturday afternoon in her snug basement that resembled a bowling alley snack bar the meeting would take place. We would find a folding chair and form a tight circle around Mrs. G's tall bar stool. She would tell who was be selected for beginning, intermediate or advanced ensemble. I fully expected to be picked for the intermediate group. I strategically sat in the chair at the end of the circle close to the corner; why should I look eager? One by one our names were called, groups were assigned and the songs to be played were announced. Forced applause was in order here. Some of the ensemble selections were unknown to us, some were pop tunes that got borderline approval, and then, my name, along with my ensemble members were announced.

"Ok, our last ensemble group will be... Charlie, Eric, Sophia, and Gretchen." Mrs. G paused and pulled out the sheet music. I moaned inside and felt my stomach cramp. I disliked all these other students. Eric Johansson was this Swedish kid from Downtown, who always smelled like fish and had warts all over his hands. He was pleasant but, I couldn't stop glaring at his warts. Sophie was a loquaciously obnoxious goodie-two-shoes. She was from Highwood; a big Italian family that loved to eat and go to mass. Ah, and then there was Gretchen, a very cute German American girl with an attitude. I would often get caught looking at her tight blouses and get a scornful death stare. Her mother was charming and beautiful; she liked me too. When she would pick Gretchen up after her lesson, she always said I was so handsome, sometimes offered me fresh baked German pastries. Of course, this drew sighs and unwanted gestures from Gretchen; secretly, I think she was smitten with me, but I'll never know.

Mrs. G now perched on her director's stool said, "Alright, gang, your music selection will be..... ummmm..... ah, yes! The beloved "LARA'S THEME", from the movie Dr. Zhivago."

We all kind of looked at each other. Sophie and Gretchen appeared happy, I tried to act happy but could only look blank. Eric looked at the floor and picked his nose, then nibbled on one of his warts. None of us knew the movie Dr. Zhivago or what is was about or the what was "Lara's Theme?"

"Mrs. G, could you sing the melody for us?" Sophie asked.

"Of course. It sounds something like this, Laaa, la, di, daaaa, la, la, la, laaaaa, di, daaa." Mrs. G sang.

"Oh yeah, I know that song!" Sophie blurted.

"Me too," shouted Gretchen.

"So, you guys happy?" Mrs. G asked.

"Oh yeah," we mumbled in chorus. Erik and I would've preferred to skip this whole competition. No chance of that now.

"Excellent, so next week I will get all the music for you guys. Remember the competition is in two months. Ensemble practices will be each Saturday Morning at 11am to noon. See you guys next week. Keep working hard on your solo music as well."

We all knew that arguing about the solo music with Mrs. G was futile. It was a crap-shoot to whom was happy with their solo music; you took the music you got, tough cheese. It was the ensemble stuff that really stressed us kids out.

Weeks went by and "Lara's Theme" sounded more minor than the key it was written in. The personality dynamics in our group was anything but complimentary. Sophie couldn't count and was always rushing. Gretchen bitched at Erik and me for not playing our parts loud enough. She did have a point; half the time I was day-dreaming and Erik just plain sucked. On occasion, Erik would pipe in with a low bass note, that sounded like a flat fart. Of course, I would start to giggle and the girls would get incensed.

We all knew what was coming with this State competition. A looming public performance. Only two weeks left to go. There was pall over us. Something that would affect all the accordionists involved. It was a sure thing. No doubt about it. We didn't want to talk or think about the stressful past group ensemble competitions, and the humiliations that had occurred and were to most likely happen again. Mrs. G referred to this dreaded terror as the Italian's from the Cicero, (a.k.a. Al Capone's hometown hideout). An accordion orchestra who took no prisoners. Their teacher and conductor, known as Dr. P, (Putalini for real) struck fear not only within her student ranks, but every freaking music teacher and participant in the downtown Chicago competition. Putalini was born in Chicago's "Little Sicily," no less. Yes, all of us from the Northshore were game to be shamed, and musically eviscerated, in public. Us kids believed that Dr. P had groomed her accordionists to employ psycho techniques to intimidate competitors like pro boxers do; stares, body posturing and yes, showmanship. It was indeed like going into a boxing ring with the infamous fighter Max Baer; death is certain. If to come back wounded, well, that could prove to make the effort worthwhile in our minds. So, to preserve the little we had to off-set a total licking, we did our best to strive forward and play "Lara's Theme" the best we could as an intermediate level accordion quartet could do. The challenge for now, gave us incentive to persevere. This was accordion war.

The first weekend in May arrived. My dad hustled me into the Oldsmobile wagon to begin the trek to the Illinois State Music Competition. As we pulled out of the driveway, my dad asked,

"Ok Chuck, got everything, your accordion, music, extra stand?

"Yep, got it all," I said while scratching my head and trying to clean the dirty lenses on my thick glasses.

"Good, let's head out then. Hope the traffic isn't bad; shouldn't be on Saturday morning."

"Yeah, I don't wanna be late." I said.

It was a gorgeous day. One of those wonderful May days that was meant to be enjoyed outdoors. The cool fresh air blew into the front seat as I lowered the window. I stuck my head out the passenger side relishing the refreshing blast of springtime air. Soon, we merged onto the expressway heading south to the Loop and then to the Mc-Cormick Place Convention Center. The smell of city traffic, along with wafts of random street vendor pastries and coffee filled the air. I loved the Chicago Loop. The L-train above Wabash hinted of the next street east, Michigan Avenue. The magic of the city helped to distract me. As we turned south on to Lake Shore Drive it wasn't long before we reached the convention center. The new McCormick Place center had just been rebuilt. It was enormous to me. It was easy to get lost in the underground parking, but my dad found a spot, only a few hundred yards from the nearest elevator. Damn, hauling my accordion wasn't fun. Dad helped me most of the time, but I wanted to show what little muscles I had; especially when girls were present. We exited the shiny new elevator to the main convention lobby. Official entrance registration tables were set up before us. Queues of music students, teachers and parents waited in line to get their status tags and performance rooms and schedules. Dad and I got in line. I looked around to see if one of my cohorts were there. Everyone there could hear the muted cacophony of accordion keys that came from the expansive hallways and multi-purpose conference rooms. As I walked up to the registration table, the stern looking official cracked a smile.

"Good morning! Your name?" the registrar asked.

"Charles Burns," I said.

"OK, I need your solo and ensemble information, oh and your teacher sponsor's name too."

"My teacher is Mrs. Ghianati. Intermediate solo, "Alfie," and…"

Oh Christ, I glanced over down the hallway and saw the Italian's from Cicero, all twelve or so of them.

"Um," I stuttered. The registrar lifted her head up to look at me directly.

"And yes, your ensemble information please." I, think she thought I was slow or something, I paused to gather my senses, and as I struggled to say what she wanted, the queen from Little Sicily, Dr. Putalini walked by the entrance tables to assemble her troop of accordion terrorists!

"Um, yeah, um… my ensemble is intermediate/advanced," I said slowly.

"And? Your ensemble music?" She asked looking down at the papers.

"Oh yeah, "Lara's Theme," I smiled.

"Ok, excellent, everything is in order Mr. Burns." She then handed me my competition name tag and my dad's visitor tag. She raised her left hand and pointed to the cavernous hallway.

"All the rooms will be down the hallway to your right. Restrooms are straight ahead and to the left."

Jesus, I felt sick. I was feeling good up till I saw the Ciceronians and Dr. P. My dad picked up my accordion and patted me on the shoulder.

"Chuck, let's use the men's room first."

"Ok," I said. I wasn't going to argue about that. Relieving myself now was a pretty good idea. As we stood side by side at the urinals, dad as usual started a conversation.

"Ok, so when is your solo time?

"Ten o'clock," I mumbled.

"How about your ensemble?"

"Not until three in the afternoon," I whined.

"Ok, then will have plenty of time for lunch." He said while staring at the bathroom wall tile, and glancing down to adjust his fly. After washing up we both fixed our hair in front of the huge lavatory mirror and began our walk to the solo area; room 129.

Our ensemble, although in the same competition category, were no match for the Ciceronians. Their fierce nemesis was the Polish group from Portage Park. The Polish kids were the accordion virtuosos from Hell! Although at least twenty ensembles competed, it was the annual duel between the Italians and the Poles that anyone really cared about. All the participants and onlookers in the performance halls could feel the impending tension. What music scores had they selected from the Music Association's official performance list? The list had intermediate to advanced scores; pop classics like "Born Free," and "Aquarius," or virtuoso classical, (the really hard stuff), pieces written by Bach, Beethoven, Mozart, and other great composers who never would have imagined their masterworks to be arranged for accordion bands.

The thick and sweaty air made it harder to focus on my solo work performance. Dad found room 129 and pointed to the door. We walked into the gray room with black plastic stack chairs neatly arranged throughout the room. The room filled quickly as the solo portion of the competition was soon to begin. Accordion cases of all levels of wear and tear lined the sides and backend of the room. Accordion cases are lined with soft velvet material with a special velvety flap that is designed to cover and protect the keyboard and bass buttons from dirt and damage. Unfortunately, this velvety material lovingly absorbs odors of the player's home practice area; garlic and onion kitchens, musty basements and other indescribable scents.

The four judges entered the room and sat behind the grading table. It got quiet.

"First soloist contestant, Mr. Sederberg, playing "Zorba," please come forward and begin. Thank you," said the one female judge. Without a word, the kid named Sederberg rose up from his back-row seat and sighed as he made his trip to the small stage, sat down, adjusted his accordion and began to play. His mother glowed with pride before he hit the first note. From then on, Sederberg's rendition of "Zorba," went from the recognizable Greek movie dance favorite to a cringe worthy staccato bastardization of musicality and melody. It was hard to watch this kid go down so badly. His mother's smile was gone. As he played the last sinful note, the room filled with parents and siblings applauded. Not because of his music, but because the misery came to an end. The judges squirmed in their chairs, saying nothing, while they made marks on the grading sheets.

"Ok, thank you," one of the older male judges said. The Sederberg kid, got up and left the stage. He smiled as he walked back to his mother. I guessed that he was relieved that the ordeal was over. That was something to smile about.

A couple more contestants came before me. One guy about my age, and a girl. Both of them played the same song, which is not unusual in competitions. She was better, perhaps because she was really cute, I wasn't listening any more. I knew I was up next. I felt sick. I hated my solo song. I had to fake this big.

"Alright, our next contestant, Mr. Burns," the stout bald adjudicator announced.

I got up, adjusted my pants, picked up my accordion from the adjoining chair and nervously wrangled my skinny arms through the instrument straps. I didn't have to bring my music sheet since it was required to play your piece by memory. God, I wanted this whole thing to be over. I walked up to the stage chair and sat down facing the silent onlookers. Jesus, the kid before me must have peed. The seat was wet and slimy.

"Oh great!" I mumbled, as I wiggled my slippery butt on the chair to find a reasonably comfortable zone near the front of the chair to rest my feet evenly on the stage floor so my accordion could rest nicely on my left thigh and right leg swung widely to the side to accommodate the bellow actions.

"Are you OK?" asked the bald judge.

"Yes sir," I reported.

"Ok, Mr. Burns, you may start anytime," the lady judge said loudly.

And so, I took a deep breath, closed my eyes to focus and played the most hated piece of music that I ever had to play. It was over before I knew it! The audience clapped. I must have done a good job. I smiled, got up took a bow and walked back to my dad who stood up and helped me take my accordion off and place it back in the case.

"Charlie, you did a great job," my dad whispered into my ear.

"Thanks dad," I said while thinking how blessed my life will be, now that I will never have to play that damn song again. I knew that my dad knew what I was thinking.

We waited for two more contestants to play. I had zoned out. Then the awards were announced.

I got third place; a yellow ribbon. I was happy.

"Ok son, on to the ensemble room for the last number."

"Yep. Lunch first, cause we still have two hours," I said.

Well, I didn't do myself any favors by eating a greasy burger and fries. This was a bad time to get nausea and gas. We finished up lunch and headed to the ensemble room.

It was a long walk. The convention center was cavernous and austere, like most. Sounds of kids and their accordions echoed through the massive hallways. I could see my quartet mates sitting on their cases near the door of the ensemble room. Erik raised his hand first to get my attention. Then Sophie, and Gretchen jumped up and pointed to me with a touch of happiness. Ms. G was standing nearby yacking with one of the other accordion teachers from another group. There was a sheet posted on the inside of the door that had been wedged open. The sheet listed the order of each ensemble group and the name of the piece they had selected to play. We all took turns to see the list. The Polish ensemble was already in the performance room warming up. Most of us were looking around for the Italians from Cicero. They were nowhere to be seen. The Ciceronians were listed to perform last. Their music selection was unrecognizable. Someone had typed over the name of the song like it was some kind of mystery for the rest of us to figure out.

"The Polish guys are playing the Hungarian Rapeseedee number two," Erik struggled to pronounce it.

"It's Rhapsody! Do you know how hard that is? Holy cow!" Sophie groaned.

"Come on," said Gretchen. "We all knew they were going to play something hard." Erik and I were trying to figure out what the tune was.

"So, what does the Hungarian song thing sound like," Erik asked sheepishly. Sophie and Gretchen both rolled their eyes.

"It's the song that they play all the time on Bugs Bunny!" Sophie said emphatically.

"You know, when Bugs is playing the piano with the orchestra."

"Yeah, the song starts with TA DAAA.... DA DA DA DAAAA, Da da da da da daaaaaa!" Gretchen sang off key. Erik and I just looked at the girls and nodded our heads in agreement. We still didn't know what the foggiest they were talking about.

We all gave up trying to figure out what the Ciceronians were going to play. No one could read it on the sheet. It read *Also spark and Beethoven V*. It was going to be a surprise I guess? It was 1:55pm, we had five minutes to show time.

We gathered our music and cases and entered the stuffy room. Everyone in the room was looking intently towards the main hallway door. It was almost time to start and the group most feared and revered were nowhere. The wall clock hit 2pm. The four judges entered, sat down and adjusted their grading sheets. Everyone lowered their voices to whispers. Just as one of the competition volunteers stood up in the back to close the door, a commotion could be heard outside the door in the hallway. Italian theatre at its best. The Cicero Accordion Academy were the best at making a spectacle. They entered the room in single file, all twelve of them, six guys, five girls and their fearless leader Dr. Putalini. The ensemble guys wore black tuxedo pants, white long sleeve ruffled shirts, black bowties, cummerbunds and polished black patent leather shoes. The girls wore long black skirts, white frilly collared blouses, black stockings and black high heels. Dr. Putalini wore her signature ivory white pant suit, gold music staff broach and white high heels. Her bleach blond hair was coiffed into a solid beehive. You couldn't miss her in Times Square during rush hour.

They marched in unison to the only seats left in the back row. The last guy wheeled in a secret weapon which appeared to be an electric bass accordion with a big ass amplifier. Erik leaned over and whispered,

"I thought those things were prohibited." I just looked at this accordion death squad with amazement.

The *"God Fatherly"* entrance was perfectly timed. The looming anxiety captivated everyone. The judges looked at one another and conversed briefly.

"Good afternoon ladies and gentlemen, welcome to the 1972 Illinois State Music competition," the stout bald judge announced firmly.

"This afternoon, we will be adjudicating ten accordion ensembles. Awards will be announced at the end of the performances today. Now, shall we begin with the first ensemble," the judge said.

"Let's see here. Yes, first contestants today will be, the Park Ridge accordion ensemble. Under the direction of Ms. Cindy Major."

This was a new cast of players that we had not seen or heard of before. The director was really young and cute. The five kids in the group made it to the stage, set up their music stands and arranged their chairs neatly into a half-moon facing the Director. Their selection was "If I Were a Rich Man." They played fine, no big screw ups except for the one kid who sat stage right and barely moved his bellows, which meant he wasn't making any sounds; probably a good thing.

Several other groups entertained the judges with tunes like, Beer Barrel Polka, Battle Hymn of The Republic, Born Free, and classics like Bach's Prelude and Fugue in D minor.

"Ok, our next group, The Lakeside Accordion players, under the direction of Ms. Ghianati, please take the stage. They will play, "Lara's Theme," the judge said.

Erik and I sat on the ends and Sophie and Gretchen sat in the middle. Ms. G raised her baton and "Lara's Theme" began. The girls were right on the beat. Erik and I, playing mostly the bass harmony were mottling through the score. Erik had a bad habit of accenting low keyboard notes that sounded more like farts than bass harmonics. Ms. G's facial expressions were super emotional; she was in her element. We could see the tears sliding down her round cheeks during the final crescendo. This motivated us to do our best. The final lingering chord produced a round of applause. Ms. G turned to face the judges and the audience and bowed. She then turned to us with a big smile and said, "Nice job kiddos!" Boy, we were so proud, even though we knew that we never had a chance of getting an award. We did it, and it was over. Now the real entertainment was to begin.

There were two more ensembles left to play. The judges shifted new grading sheets on the table, and whispered to each other. The defending champs were Italians from Cicero. Their only competition and nemesis were the Poles from the neighborhood nearby.

"And now, the ensemble from the Portage Park Accordion Academy, under the direction of Edvard Kasianaslovski, will play Hungarian Rhapsody No. 2 in D Minor by Franz Liszt," the lady judge announced.

We could all hear the other contestants mumble words like "Oh wow," or "OOOOOhhhh." The Ciceronans in the back remained stone-faced, as did Dr. Putalini. The PPAA ensemble, ten kids in all, six guys and four girls, all teen-agers took their performance positions. To be different, the girls sat in front and the guys stood in a half-moon line behind the girls. Mr. Kasianaslovski, who stood about five-foot four inches with his black two-inch lift ankle boots, stepped forward to take his conductor position. Just as he raised his baton, and all attention was glued, someone in the back row, tooted loudly. We all suspected it was one of the PPAA's rivals from Cicero. However, the battle began.

Kasianaslovski, with great defiance whipped his baton to accent the first explosive chord.

"TA DAaaaaa, Da, Da, Da DAAAA, Ta, Da, Daaaaa, Da Ta Daaaaa...."

And so, it began. Kasianaslovski and his students gave this classic score a remarkable new sound. The clarity, speed and agility of these accordionists was inspiring. The judges, normally pokerfaced could be seen head rocking and toe tapping. We were all consumed by the joyful Rhapsody and how delightfully this group played it. The final five accented chords brought the piece to an end, along with a standing ovation. Some of us kids looked back at the smug Cicero kids and Dr. Pusalini who only acknowledged the perfect performance with wet fish hand claps.

Once Kasianaslovski's group humbly left the stage, two of the competition volunteers were requested to arrange the stage chairs by Dr. Putalini.

"And now, our final ensemble for the competition is The Cicero Accordion Academy, under the direction of Dr. Cara Putalini. Their selection will be a medley featuring Richard Strauss and Beethoven, selections from Also Sprach Zara Thustra and Beethoven's Fifth Symphony."

The CAA entourage marched up to the stage, each player choreographed to take their performance positions. A guy who wheeled up the heavy amp and electric accordion bass, quickly hooked up the system on stage right. Dr. Putalini called him Guido.

"Guido, set the volume," said Dr. Putalini in her low raspy voice. Guido played a short arpeggio on the bass keyboard. It was impressively commanding. Guido, nodded to Dr. Putalini.

Dr. Putalini reached up for her conductor's baton which was sticking out of her beehive doo. She pulled it out like a dagger. She raised her arms high and the players placed their hands at attention on their treble and bass keyboards. All her players were at supreme attention but never let go of their *Don Corleone* stares. The fight for accordion champs was in the making.

"BAMmmmmmmm, BAmmmmmm, Bammmmmm, bammm mmm.....Bam, Bammmmmmmm!" Guido pounded on the electric bass accordion. The whole band pumped their bellows in to blow out the triple forte chords in unison.

"BAM, Bam, bammmm, Bammmmm, Bammmmmmmmmmmm!"

The thunderous jolts shook the room. Richard Strauss' excerpt, Also Sprach Zara Thustra, otherwise known as the "2001 Space Odyssey" theme song as their intro drew immediate applause and audible approval. Then it ended. Total silence. The audience was in a trance.

Putalini brought her arms down to her sides and lowered her chin. Her players paused.

They turned the pages of their music sheets, and quickly resumed hand positions. Putalini, wielding her baton like a rapier, raised both arms to the ceiling. She threw her arms down and the flood of mind-blowing, earth shaking notes hit us in the face like the wind of a nuclear blast; vulgar but awesome! DA, DA, DA,DAAAAaaa aaaaa....DA,DA, DA, DAaaaaaa....! It was brash perfection. Gauche and inspiring at the same time! Quite frankly, it was, what everyone had expected from this troupe of Westside accordion fame. The fast and furious finger work on both treble and bass boards, was freaking mind blowing. The four girls in the center playing treble parts made magical harmony with the guys in the back row working the bass lines. Guido was in a league all his own. Pumping the hell out of the huge electrified monster bellows he cradled between his massive thunder thighs. The passion was contagious. The judges fell back in their chairs and closed their eyes as if they were having out of body experiences. There wasn't a soul in the room that wasn't smiling at this totally out-of-this world accordion experience. The Beethoven crescendo approached. Putalini wildly gesticulated her arms and torso making her beehive lean back and forth as if the Tower of Pisa was earth-shaken. This was what everyone waited for all year long. No one was disappointed. The final keys were pressed in one massive chord. Before Putalini brought her arms to accent the finale of Beethoven's masterpiece, the eruptive applause filled the room. Indeed, the best was saved for last! The feared accordion gang from Cicero received the standing ovation they deserved. At this point, all the other contestants didn't give a damn how they placed. All of us knew who the winner was, and it was the CAA! Bravo, parents chanted. Putalini, turned to face the adoring crowd, took a bow and signaled to her troupe to all stand and bow. The performers all smiled, even Guido could be seen grinning, his chubby face expanding to a half moon. Putalini neatly returned her magic baton into her beehive. The war was over, jubilantly! The CAA were awarded First Place, The Poles got second for their Hungarian Rhapsody, and a group from Shaumburg got third place for their rendition of "The Blue Danube." We got an honorable mention. Ms. G was ecstatic. She cried as she hugged all of us. We could all now take a deep breath and think about summer. As for my solo sheet music, "Alfie," it was never seen again.

Kudos to my childhood accordion dudes: Myron Floren who brought the accordion into America's living room, Billy Joel who made the accordion cool and Weird Al Yankovic who gave the accordion a pop twist. Too many great players out there! Thanks to my dear departed Aunt Margie for lighting the spark.

09/2023 KJ Lawlor All Rights Reserved "Accordion Wars."

Forever Tenderfoot

"Ok scouts," Scoutmaster Erikson shouted. "Time to present the merit badges for the month." The gathering of about thirty guys, ages eleven to seventeen lined up against the gym wall and sat down. We were required to wear our official scout uniforms. My uniform was brand new. I should've washed it a few times to make it look more rugged. I looked too neat.

I joined the Boy Scouts at the beginning of seventh grade. I was talked into it by my neighbor Morgan Melton. I was the smallest kid in the school district. I thought joining would boost my image. To me, it was something a tough guy should do.

Morgan did a great sales job. He showed me his scouting uniforms, hats and camping gear. He talked about the adventures of being in the woods, shooting rifles and cooking meals over the camp fire. He recruited me into Forest Bluff Troop #42 in the Fall of 1972. I had joined a month earlier and attended two scout workshops: basic first aid, knot tying, and campfire safety. I had spent the previous weekend at my first official campout. To be honest, I didn't find it enjoyable. Sleeping in pup tents in the rain was not my idea of fun or being tough. I went along with the group, for now. I wanted to give this new activity some more time to sink in. It could get better? This evening I was to receive my first badge, Tenderfoot. I was so excited. I put the rain-soaked memory out of mind. The badges were doled out by Troop number and names alphabetically. My troop was called first.

"Charlie Burns," said Scout Master Erikson. I stood up awkwardly, my butt was numbed. I limped up to the presenting Scout Master. He ceremoniously shook my hand.

"Scout Burns, you have earned the official rank of Tenderfoot Scout," the Scout Master announced. He then pinned the shiny Tenderfoot medal on my shirt pocket. Everyone clapped. I turned around to face my fellow scouts and smiled. Being shy, I felt out of place as a beginner scout.

"Way to go Charlie," yelled Morgan.

"Woo ho," other attendees hollered while clapping in slow chimp-like motions, like they could have cared less. The badge presentations continued for another 15 minutes. Then our Troop Scout Master made the big announcement about the Winter campout plans. This was a big deal; a scout requirement to get to the next badge rank, for me it would be Scout Second Class. I wanted to make it to Scout First Class by next Spring.

"Ok boys, the Winter campout weekend is planned for the second weekend in February," said the Scout Master reading from his clipboard.

"Ooh Yeah," yelled a few older scouts.

"We're all going to Camp Chiwacatagotah near Rockford," Erikson said.

"The camp has log cabins and well-equipped (out-houses) facilities as well as five miles of hiking trails." I thought about this mid-winter adventure with reservation.

"Boys, get with your Troop leaders and organize your Chiwacatogotah camping plans," said the Scout Master.

"Ok, that wraps it up. Next time we meet will be at Chiwacatogotah!"

All of us erupted into a half-assed applause. I guess I wasn't the only scout considering the 'not-fun-element' to this trip. We broke up into our troop group assignments. Our troop division had six guys. The head scout called the shots. His name was Grant Windsor. He had a twin brother Stewart. Grant and Stewart planned for the pre-camp meeting to be held at their home a few weeks before the camp-out.

"Gentlemen," said Grant, "During our pre-camp meeting we will discuss preparations such as food and beverages, winter gear and of course transportation to the camp." Stewart stood next to his twin brother and nodded in approval.

"Stewart will call you to let you know the day and time," said Grant.

Grant and Stewart stood six-foot tall, skinny with thick jet-black hair tightly cropped. They smelled like their clothes had been washed and pressed in pleasant cologne. They didn't seem to fit the rough and tumble image of scouting. They looked more like models for a Chanel ad.

"Sounds good to me," said Morgan.

"Yep," mumbled the rest of us.

"We will see you gentlemen next month," Grant said as we all waved good-bye and left the gym.

A few weeks into January, Morgan and I arrived at Grant and Stewart's home. Morgan's Dad gave us a ride. He wasn't sure he was at the right address. It was almost 6:30pm and dark. The freshly plowed entrance driveway to their estate was several hundred feet long.

"Is this the right house?" Morgan's Dad asked.

"Yep, it is," said Morgan. "See, it says 'Windsor' on the mailbox. Windsor is their last name," Morgan said as he pointed to the mailbox. His Dad drove us up to the front walkway. Morgan and I wiggled out of the back seat and headed to the front door.

"Wow, what a huge house," I said. "I mean, this is a mansion. These guys are super rich." Morgan rang the doorbell. I felt like Oliver Twist standing in the cold.

Mrs. Windsor let us in. We took off our coats and hung them on the wall hooks, then yanked off our boots. The house smelled like the twins, a scent of a freshly opened bar of expensive soap. No garlic and onion odors in this place.

We walked into the master den. The entire room was white, even the plush carpet. Steve, Billy and Doug were already sitting on the floor with legs crossed.

"Grant and Stewart will be down in a minute. They just got back from the club. Would you gentleman like to have some butterscotch cookies and milk?" asked Mrs. Windsor.

"Yes, Mrs. Windsor," said Steve. We all nodded and smiled.

"That's splendid. I'll have the maid bring your cookies and milk right away," she said as she left the room. We all looked at each other in silence, and Steve whispered, "They got a maid." We all sat quietly looking around the white den, afraid to touch anything. The maid entered the room. She held up a tray with five glasses of milk and a plate stacked with cookies.

"Hello boys, here is your milk and cookies," she said. We all smiled in approval.

As the maid exited the den, the twins entered, wearing their tennis whites.

"Good evening gentlemen," Grant said.

"Yes, evening scouts," Stewart followed.

"Hi guys," Said Steve. We all raised our hands to wave. Grant and Stewart pulled up two office chairs and set them behind the coffee table in front of us. Grant held a folder emblazoned with the official seal of Boys Scouts of America. We all sat watching Grant turn the pages to review camping plan protocols. I noticed he had a milk mustache and some cookie crumbs on his tennis polo. It looked like he was unprepared for this meeting and was pulling words from his ass.

"Yes, so gentlemen," Grant said. "I will now delegate who will be in charge of specific duties for the up-coming Winter camp out." He paused waiting for some kind of group acknowledgement. We all just sat like toads looking at him.

"So, Ok, let's see?" Grant said awkwardly.

"Billy Metzger, you are in charge of organizing meal provisions."

"Ok," Billy said.

"This means having four meals prepared for each of us," Grant said.

Doug was chosen to gather camp gear. Since we were going to have cabins, all he needed to get were flashlights, paper plates, napkins and toilet paper. Morgan was told to be in charge of scout safety and fire rules.

I was designated to provide drinks.

"And finally, Steve Knutson, you will be in charge of transportation to and from camp Chiwacatogotah," said Grant.

"Oh, perfect," said Steve. "My Dad has a VW bus, it'll be great for the trip! It carries up to nine passengers and tons of room for everything else."

Grants' poker face pinched.

"How old is the VW bus?" Grant asked.

"It's a 1967, in great condition," Steve said, "Why?"

Grant and Stewart's thick black eyebrows scrunched in disapproval.

"Well," Grant said briefly clearing his throat of cookie crumbs, "My father told me that VW buses, or hippie vans, are not road worthy and are unsafe."

"What?" Steve said, "The VW bus is reliable, and it's safe.

"It's a nice micro-bus," added Billy, "My dad rides to gigs in Mr. Knutson's van all the time. They play in a band together on the weekends."

Grant searched for what to say and leaned in to consult with Stewart. They whispered inaudibly. Grant turned back to face us.

"Alright, Steve and the rest of you can ride in the VW bus with the supplies. Stewart and I will ride in our Mom's Cadillac. We will have room for one of you in the Deville should you choose not to ride in the Knutson's VW." We all just sat dumb founded. Looked at one another, like wow, what a couple of dicks.

"Anyone want to ride with us?" Grant asked.

No one raised their hand or made a peep. From that moment on, this whole camping venture was off to a bad start.

I thought, "Wow, tough guys, sure?"

"OK gentlemen, that does it for tonight," Grant said while closing the manual in front of him. "Stewart will call you a week before the camp out to see if you have your designated tasks in hand."

We all got up, went to put on our boots and coats and left the house to stand at the edge of the driveway. We left with a bad impression. Our Troop leaders had pissed in our cornflakes.

Stewart called me a week before the drive to camp Chiwacatogotah.

"So, Charlie, you are in charge of beverages, right?" Stewart asked.

"Yep," I said. "I am bringing six gallons of water, two twelve packs of soda, and six big bottles of juice."

"What kind of juice?" asked Stewart.

"Prune juice," I said jokingly, but he obviously didn't get it.

"No, just kidding, it's apple and grape," I said.

"Oh yeah, ha, ok, well that's good," Stewart said. "You have the map information?

"Yep," I said. "We'll meet you guys at the camp next Saturday morning at ten."

"Sounds good, Burns, we'll see you there," Stewart said.

I had gathered all my winter camping clothes, sleeping bag and cardboard boxes loaded with drinks. I waited by the door peeking out every couple of minutes to see if the VW bus was coming down the street. It was bitter cold. The wind chill made it worse. I thought of the adventure and nice log cabins. I looked at my scout watch. Steve's dad was late. I opened the door a crack again to peer outside. I could see Morgan with his hiking-pack trudging up our driveway.

"Hey Morgan," I yelled. "They're late."

Morgan made his way up the stoop, then dumped his pack on the stairs.

"They should be here, where are they?" Morgan complained while smearing the fog off his horn-rim glasses. The wind blew hard making it difficult to see or hear.

"We're gonna be late! We'll miss the orientation," he whined just as a gust of wind hit him in the face with a helping of snow.

I looked up and could hear the Mr. Knutson's VW shifting at the stop sign on the corner.

"Here they come," I said. Morgan turned around to watch the van come up the drive. Steve jumped out of the side door of the van.

"Hey guys," he called out. "let's load the stuff in the back." Steve then raised the back gate. We shoved the drinks, hiking packs and sleeping bags in the luggage compartment and all climbed in.

"Oh God, it's so nice and warm in here," I said. Mr. Knutson smiled and nodded while looking at the rearview mirror.

"Yeah, feels good," Morgan added. He couldn't see crap through his fogged lenses and struggled to find the seat belt.

"I love this van," said Billy sitting close to one of the floor heater vents.

"So, do I," said Doug jammed in the middle seat dressed like Nanook of the North. The VW van was great. It was the symbol of outdoor recreation. Nothing like a VW micro-bus. The weather was horrible, but we didn't care. We were toasty warm and ready to earn our next level badges.

"Looks like we're here boys," Mr. Knutson announced. He slowed the bus down to veer into the rocky off-road entrance to Camp Chi-wacatogotah.

"Well boys, I can only drive this far. The snow is too deep. You guys can hike to the scout cabins." He pointed to the cabin behind some trees.

"Let's go guys," Steve said. We all stepped out of the van trying not to fall over each other.

"Man, I gotta piss," moaned Doug.

"Me too," said Billy.

"Shut up!" said Morgan, "the out-houses are behind the Scout Master's cabin." We got all our provisions and gear out of the van. Steve brought his 'Flyer' sled with a rope. We stacked the drink boxes on it. All loaded up, we waved to Mr. Knutson and he carefully backed up.

"See you boys tomorrow afternoon," he smiled, then drove off. We marched in slow-motion, pulling our sled up to the entrance gate. The signage above the road resembled a German stalag.

Welcome to 'C mp hi acatog t h.'

"What the heck does that say?" Steve said.

"Welcome to frozen hell," I laughed.

"Where are the prison quarters," Billy said laughing.

We all heard the snow crunching from another car pulling up to the camp from the highway.

"Well, look who's here!" Steve said with a sneer.

"Oh lord, it's the twins," Billy said.

The jet-black Cadillac drove through the deep unplowed snow like a tank. The car came within a few feet of the gate.

We could see the twins in the back seat. Their mother talked to them without turning her head. The passenger doors opened slowly and Grant and Stewart got out. The twins carefully removed their weekend gear. They wiggled into their back packs. Mrs. Windsor backed up on the tracks she had made. She got stuck at one point, but a couple of the Scout Masters who had pulled in behind her managed to help her maneuver the beastly car out of the rut. Grant and Stewart, dressed in expensive winter outer wear, walked toward us. We waited for them.

"Greetings, troop leaders," Steve said, bowing his head. We raised our hands to be polite.

"Looks like we're all here." Grant said while doing a manual head count.

"Ok, good, let's go to the main cabin. We'll get our lodging assignments."

We all headed to the main camp headquarters. We followed Grant and Stewart up to the doors of the headquarters.

"Gentlemen, stay out here," Grant said. "I'll go in to find out what cabin you are going to be in." Stewart followed his brother and closed the door behind him. The wind got stronger and colder.

"Nice!" said Steve. "We get the pleasure of waiting out here in the frozen tundra." We all were tired of carrying our supplies. We dropped the heavy back packs and sat on them. After about five minutes, which seemed like an hour, Grant stuck his head out the doorway.

"Ok gentlemen, you're sharing cabin number two with Troop 46 from Elgin," said Grant. He extended his arm to point to the cabin two, about two hundred feet from where we stood.

"Your Scout Master will be Mr. Hogan," Grant reported. "Due to the bad weather, all the outdoor activities are cancelled until tomorrow AM." He closed the door.

Steve led the way to the cabin. The closer we got, the worse it looked. One of the porch posts had buckled from rot. The only front window was smashed and boarded up. Steve and I walked up to the door and took turns trying to open it.

"Jesus Christ," Steve said. After a couple of coordinated yanks, the door opened. The other troop hadn't shown up yet. We all dragged our belongings into the cold and dark log cabin.

"Oh shit! What a dump," Billy said.

"Yeah, right," Doug added.

"What did you expect, you babies, the Taj Mahal?" Morgan said like tough guy. I agreed with Steve, Billy and Doug. Morgan was full of crap.

The cabin stunk; odors of moldy socks, rotten spam and wet burned firewood. There were six-bunk beds in the one room cabin, a fireplace covered with cob webs and a pile of fire wood in the corner. The combination of foul odors and dust made it hard to breathe. Just as the tribal bitching was to continue, Scout Master Hogan arrived.

"Hello scouts, I'm Mr. Hogan," he said cheerfully.

"Hi, Mr. Hogan, Scout Master..." we all mumbled.

"Nice cabin, let's get a fire started boys."

"Yes, I know the place is a little dirty, but it's better than sleeping out in the blizzard," Mr. Hogan joked. "Have you guys picked out your bunks? Better do it before the other troop gets here." We all looked at one another for bunk mates. Steve and I got the bunk closet to the cabin door. Doug and Billy got the one next to us. Morgan and Mr. H picked the one near the fireplace. About an hour later, the Troop from Elgin which was unknown to us arrived. We watched their faces droop in disgust as they entered the weekend lodging.

"Welcome Troop forty-six from Elgin!" Steve announced.

"A home away from home," Steve laughed.

The guys all smirked. They weren't happy either. You could tell what they were thinking.

Mr. Hogan and Morgan had got the fireplace roaring. The heat from the fire helped to ease the biting cold and brighten up the dingy space. We all took turns standing by the fireplace. Mr. Hogan sat on the only chair in the cabin, an old rickety rocker. It was too cold to do much of anything. The priority was to stay warm. When dinner time came around, hotdogs were roasted over the fire, placed on ice cold buns and consumed with canned beans. Everyone got a cold drink and a frozen Twinkie for dessert. No one complained.

"Well boys, the winter survival talk is early tomorrow morning at 7am," Mr. Hogan said. "Time to get some sleep." Mr. Hogan just sat in the old rocker by the fire place, his fat belly stretching his olive-green sweater over his belt. I could see his bald head shine from the glow of the fire leaning back on the rocker with both chubby legs fully extended toward the warmth. He had a big smile on his face. Sure, he was warm.

"Hey Charlie," Steve called from the bottom bunk.

"What?" I said.

"How is it up there?" said Steve

"I'm freezing," I said.

"Me too," he said.

We were both fully dressed, wearing wool hats and gloves while stuffed into our Sears cowboy printed sleeping bags. I stared at the filthy wooden ceiling. I knew that to get my Second-Class Scout badge, this was the crap I had to endure. I didn't feel one bit tougher. I thought about my warm bed and indoor plumbing. I dreamed of a hot breakfast, pancakes and sausage. It was Saturday night. I missed watching 'Mutual of Omaha's Wild Kingdom' and 'Walt Disney Presents' on our new color TV. The more I thought of these pleasures, the less I cared about badges. I could see my breath. I turned my head to glance at Mr. Hogan enjoying the fire and seeing the other guys squirming in their sleeping bag misery. I started to get sleepy and remembered hearing a mountain climber guy say that people don't feel much when they freeze to death, they just fall asleep. These thoughts didn't help. I looked at my scout watch. It was around 9pm. I left my glasses on, closed my eyes and hoped for the best.

I woke to the sound of coughing and smell of smoldering ashes. A billowing column of grey smoke was flowing out of the fireplace to the ceiling. I furiously kicked and pulled my body out of the sleeping bag. I grabbed the top end post of the bunk, missed the ladder and fell hard onto the floor. I splintered up my palm on the unfinished wood rail. I stood up and could see the smoke getting thicker and lower to the floor. The guys on the top bunks were suffocating. I bolted to the only working door in the cabin, threw back the latch and kicked it open. A welcome blast of fresh air hit my face. I scrambled to the fire place were Mr. Hogan was snoring loudly and in a state of hibernation. I remembered dad always telling me about the fireplace flue. Instinct took over. I grabbed the log poker lying next to Mr. Hogan's rocker. I covered my nose and mouth with the collar of my turtle neck. I jammed the soot covered poker into the base of the flue. It was like trying to thread a needle blindfolded. The poker got stuck. It had to be the flue hatch?

"Jesus Christ," I yelled. "Goddamn it!"

I then pushed the end of the poker up. The flue hatch opened and I could feel it lock open. The smoke reversed its flow. The air was clearing.

"What the Hell are you doing?" yelled the Mr. Hogan still stuck to his rocker.

"Why is the door open? It's freezing!" I didn't say anything to him. I just looked passed him, clapped the soot off my hands and went to close the door. The coughing slowed down as the room cleared of the deadly fumes.

The weirdest thing is that all the guys fell back asleep. Even Mr. Hogan returned to hibernation. He had screwed up. Fell asleep on duty. Best not to talk about it, right? All's well that ends well. I returned to my bunk. I felt like a soldier who just saved his platoon from an ambush. For a moment, I thought of myself as a hero. But that wasn't what I wanted to be. I wanted to be warm, have a hot pancake breakfast and be anywhere but in this dirty, cold and forgettable place.

I woke up around five AM. The fire needed more logs but was burning as it should. Everyone in the cabin was still sleeping. Mr. Hogan had moved to one of the open bunks. So much for tending the fire. Could last night have been a dream? No, the big splinter in my hand reminded me.

I unzipped my cowboy sleeping bag and climbed down the bunk ladder, put my boots and coat on and quietly left the cabin. The winter sunrise was beautiful. I walked on trails of fresh wind-carved drifts then sat on a camp bench to catch sun's first beams to light up the snow. I wondered why I was here?

"To get your Second Class BSA badge," I told myself. The truth was that I just saved two scout troops and an incompetent Scout Master from dying from smoke inhalation. I thought about the aftermath had I not jumped into action. All the dead boys and an overfed bear toasted on the floor. I realized that I was already self-reliant. My deeds were above and beyond any scout badges.

I got back to the cabin. I opened the door and smelled something burning. It was Mr. Hogan whipping up some camp grub. Spam and French toast on Coleman portable grill.

"Shouldn't he be cooking that crap outside?" I thought.

"Hey Charlie, where have you been?" Steve asked sipping a Coke.

"Oh, just out on the trails," I said.

"Did you hear that the winter survival activities were cancelled," said Steve.

"Really. Why," I said.

"It's too cold! Ha," he laughed, along with the others.

"Get it? Too cold for winter survi.."

"Yeah, I get it," I said with a smile.

The big winter camp weekend at 'Chiwacotagotah' was a bomb. Our parents were notified of the cancellation from the local BSA office in Rockford. They told that we needed to be picked up earlier than expected. Mr. Knutson's VW arrived to take us home. I was so happy. Steve, Billy, Doug and I loaded all the gear and leftover provisions into the back trunk. I was the last one to step into the side passenger door. I turned around to watch Morgan, Grant and Stewart get into the Cadillac. Morgan was obviously brown nosing the higher ranks and opted to take the vacant seat offered on the Windsor's limo. "Tough guys," I thought? I then looked over to the dilapidated camp sign, 'C mp hi acatog t h.' I stood at attention, raised my right hand in the Boy Scout salute.

"Forever Tenderfoot," I shouted gleefully. Steve tugged the back of my coat.

"Get your ass in the van. It's freezing!"

Death and Candy

On an Indian summer morning, two weeks before the coveted Halloween night, my sister Ellie reached for the ringing kitchen wall phone. There was a short silence after she said "Hello," followed by a gasp and "Suzy, you ok?" I watched her turn pale.

"God, that's so horrible! Where did they find her? Oh God, this is horrible." I could tell Ellie was trying not to cry. I knew that someone was dead.

"I just saw Alex yesterday at school," Ellie said. "Kristen must have been alone?"

"Ok, I'll let everyone know. Thanks, bye," Ellie turned to me. "Man, oh man, you're not gonna believe what Suzy just heard." Her voice shaking she walked over to the kitchen island and sat down on a stool. For a few moments, she couldn't speak. Pressing her hands against the sides of her head, she slumped over the counter. I stuffed the end of a Hostess Ding Dong in my mouth and followed it with a slug of cold milk.

"You know Kristen Lundquist?"

"Yeah, she's in eighth. I only see her at PE," I said.

"She was murdered last night. After school. In their living room."

"No way?" I said.

"It's true. Kristen's mom found her. Don't know how she was killed."

I shook my head. "Did they get the guy?"

"No, and this is so scary. Now there's a killer on the loose."

The phone rang again. Ellie picked it up, her voice cracking. "5388,"

I could hear mom's high-pitched voice coming from the earpiece of the phone. Mom was a librarian and always heard the latest gossip from her assistant, Mrs. Lindenmeyer, who knows everything and everybody in Forest Bluff.

"What? Really? Oh god. Ok, I'll lock the doors. See you soon." Ellie hung up. She snapped the lock on the kitchen door and headed for the living room. Five seconds later I heard the snap of another lock. I could feel my hands shaking.

Things like this just didn't happen were we lived. A killer was on the run in Forest Bluff, Illinois. We found out that this sweet kid, Kristen Lundquist, was bludgeoned to death when she came home from school. The police had no suspects, and they couldn't find the murder weapon. Everyone was scared. And yet, us elementary and junior high kids knew what was on the line. Death wasn't easy for elementary kids to process, understandably. The finality of death was fuzzy. Us kids deserved to know more, but were so often left out because of social taboos. Death was a mystery to most of us. One day you're sitting next to a kid in the lunch room, and the next day you find out on the playground that the same kid was shot and killed accidentally at home. No adults would talk about these things. Did the parents and teachers think that we were stupid? Like sex education, we had to figure it out by ourselves.

Days went by and still no suspects. The killing, now locally known as the Lundquist murder, was the talk of the town. Normally this time of year, we talked about the world series, how burning leaves was bad for the environment and who got the biggest pumpkin. This autumn had no comparison in Forest Bluff. We, the kids, knew where this was going.

A week before Halloween, the city authorities and police chief gathered for a town forum and formally cancelled Halloween. While we were sad about Kristen Lundquist, we saw this differently. No way was our Halloween going to be cancelled. Halloween was fun and fruitful. We spent weeks planning our costuming and trick or treat routes, whose house in the neighborhood was the scariest and who dished out the best goods. Valentines and Easter couldn't measure up to Halloween. The weather didn't matter. Rain, snow, hot, cold, the mission of reaping pounds of candy was at hand.

The following Monday morning, the school yard was buzzing with kids talking about the murder and cancellation of Halloween. My neighbor and best friend Ernie had a plan to thwart the City Council's decision. He sat on one the playground benches and chewed on handfuls of Sweet Tarts. Ernie and I both had coke-bottle-bottom eyeglasses. His black hair was neatly combed, but greasy. His husky build and doughy appearance disqualified him as a babe magnet. I didn't qualify either. I was the smallest kid in the school district, had braces and the first kid in my group to get zits. Ernie wasn't popular, and neither was I. We were nerdy. In spite of the Lundquist murder, we wanted our Halloween and the large caches of candy that go with it. So did every other kid in Forest Bluff.

"Ok, Chuck, here's my plan," Ernie said. I just looked at him and sat down on the bench.

"Ok, listen, this is perfect!"

"I'm listening," I said.

"Look, if we can get some inside leads to help the cops get this guy, Halloween can be saved," Ernie said sharply.

"Sure, what leads?" I quizzed.

"It's pretty simple," Ernie said.

"What do you mean simple?

"Ok, listen, it's gotta be someone the family knows. No forced entry; nothing stolen. I mean come on!"

"And?" I asked.

"We just need to do some inside detective stuff, but we don't have a lot of time," said Ernie. I stared at him.

"You're nuts. Who's going to help us with that?" I blurted.

"Look, at this." Ernie handed me his old wrinkled math test. I took it.

"Sure, another A+. What's that supposed to mean, smarty pants?"

Ernie sighed, and pointed to the bottom of the test paper.

There, in his chicken-scratch notes he had written three names: *Suzy M, Ellie and Mrs. Lindenmyer.* This was to be our team of sleuths, plus Ernie and me. Our mission was to get crucial information about Kristen's circle of family and friends. Then slip the notes to the police, and help them apprehend the killer.

I went along with Ernie's plan. I thought it was a long shot, but we had nothing to lose. Ernie gave me several things to do. I had to get Ellie to call Mrs. Lindenmyer and Suzy Mullins to get any news about the Lundquists. He also wanted me to bike to Kristen's neighborhood and check out the house. I had been practicing typing with Dad's old portable manual Smith Corona. My notes needed to be readable for Ellie:

```
Ask Mrs. Lindenmyer: Who are their friends?
Any people who don't like them? How well
```

do you know the kids? What happened to the
father?

Ask Suzy: Your sister dated her brother, is
he a nice guy? What did he talk to your sister
about? Where did they go for dates? When and
why did they break up?

I was sure that Ellie could come up with more questions, but this
was a start; first I had to ask Ellie to join our mission. Her task was
to visit Mrs. Lindenmyer at the library and get some gossip about
the Lundquist family and call her friend Suzy whose older sister had
gone to the Junior prom with Kristen Lundquist's older brother Alex.
Girlfriend's sharing secrets about sibling's dating news shouldn't be
too hard, especially with Suzy Mullins. After a little chiding, she agreed
to assist, but not without a catch; I had to do her house chores for
a month. This harmless detective work was right up her ally. While
Ellie, Ernie and I knew what the goal was here, Mrs. Lindenmyer and
Suzy Mullins did not, we had to keep all the interrogations appear
as simple gossip and nothing more. Once I collected the information
requested of Ellie from Mrs. Lindenmyer and Suzy, Ernie and I could
start putting some of the parts of the puzzle together. Ernie was the
logistics man. Next thing was to get on my bike and do some on the
road investigation around the Lundquist property and the homes of
possible suspects.

I gave Ellie the list of topics to discuss with Mrs. Lindenmyer and
Suzi Mullins. Ellie was a good conversationalist; however, even so, the
milking of sensitive and dually private gossip had to be done delicately.
This would be easy with Mrs. Lindenmyer who loved to yack freely
about anyone or anything, but Suzy not so much, she was tight lipped
about most things unless it was about boys.

The Lundquist home was about a ten-minute bike ride from our house. The chilly air and strong breeze made the trip uncomfortable. I rode around the Lundquist's neighborhood making several passes by their house. I felt weird doing it, and stopped several times pretending that my pedal gears weren't working so that I didn't look suspicious. The driveway was empty, leaves covered the yard and the front walk. I couldn't help but imagine Kristen walking into the house for the last time. The horror that awaited her. I stopped at the end of the block to pan the area. As I checked my watch for the time, a red Pontiac Trans Am pulled around the corner and crawled into the Lundquist driveway and their automatic garage door opened. The car stopped, shifted to neutral, the engine revved up, then pulled in slowly. There was a silver 1957 Corvette parked in the two-car garage. I had never seen that car before. I watched out of the corner of my eye and saw Alex Lundquist exit the Trans Am, stop and look back at the polished Corvette, then casually take out his house key and enter the backdoor. For a moment, I really got creeped out. I sped home as the sun began to set.

After school the next day, Ellie went to the city library to visit mom and strike up a little gossip with Mrs. Lindenmyer. When Ellie got home, she ran in the kitchen almost out of breath.

As I sat eating my Hostess Ding Dong with a tall glass of milk, she tossed down her book bag on the floor and plopped down in the seat next to me.

"Look what I got!" she proclaimed with glee.

"What?" I said.

"I got Mrs. Lindenmyer singing like a bird. I mean she had so much to say about Kristen's family."

"Anything good?" I said.

"Are you kidding me? Look, here is what she told me about the Lundquists, I wrote it all down." Ellie said holding the notes in front of her. I rested my elbows on the table and rested my chin on my fists as I listened to her report.

"And...?" I asked.

"Ok, listen to this. Kristen's mother works for a medical company in Northbrook, the dad was a wealthy architect and died three years ago; heart attack. While Kristen got along with her parents, there was a lot of friction with Alex. Mrs. Lindenmyer said that Kristen's mom would meet her after church on Sundays and have coffee. She would tell her about all the problems with Alex. His grades were slipping, which she thought had to do with losing his father, but there was more to the story. Alex hangs around with a strange guy who works on cars; Um, Barney, something. They mess around with old muscle cars. You know Barney Butthead from school, right?"

"Yeah, sort of." I thought hard.

"He's a burnout, a former senior drop-out that hangs around the high school mechanic shop. Yeah, I know that guy," Ellie said.

"I don't know him, just seen him park his old green Dog Fart (Dodge Dart) in front of Forest Bakery. Yeah, practically every morning like clockwork he's there. He's goofy and always wears black. I think his dad died when Barney was little."

"Yeah, he's strange," Ellie added. "Shankles! Barney Shankles! That's his name." Ellie shouted.

"What else?" I asked.

"Ok, so the father apparently had an enormous life insurance policy. Kristen's mom is very rich! She had told Mrs. Lindenmyer that she didn't need to work, but wants to keep working to keep her sanity. So, there it is."

"Don't know if there's any leads with this, but I will pass it on to Ernie," I said taking Ellie's notes from her hands.

"Next, I am calling Suzy to find out more about her sister dating Alex," Ellie said as she stood up. She picked up the receiver from the wall phone, stretched out the twisted cord, and diced up Suzy's number. Ellie purposely held the receiver away from her ear so I could hear. I pulled up a chair closer to Ellie to hear better. Ellie shushed me for making too much noise.

"Hello,"

"Hi, is this Mrs. Mullins?"

"Yes Ellie, I'll get Suzy." Mrs. Mullins said softly.

"Hey Ellie, what's up kiddo?" Suzy asked.

"Not much, just wanted to say hi and ask if you got a lot of homework from English class today?" Ellie asked but was thinking about her next words.

"Well, Dr. Conway really didn't give us much to do except research the Latin roots for a bunch of vocab stuff," Suzy reported.

"Hey, didn't Linda have Dr. Conway last year in Junior English Lit? Wasn't Alex Lundquist in that class too," Ellie jumped right to it. My sister didn't mess around. Always to the point. I leaned in a little closer to Ellie, she raised her hand in a fist, then made a *don't screw with me face* gesture.

"Yeah, she did have Conway last year, and yeah, that's where Linda met Alex. Why?" said Suzy. I wanted to laugh, but knew if I did, Ellie would let me have it.

"Well, I just thought about Alex because of his sister's murder and stuff and wondered if Linda has heard anything from him?" Ellie said trying to be careful.

"Linda broke up with Alex months ago. I thought you knew that?" Suzy quipped. I shook my head melodramatically.

"I kinda knew that, but wasn't sure. So why did they break up? Did he do something bad?" Ellie pried.

"Linda secretly told me, and this is just between you and me, right?" Suzy said. I placed my hands over my head.

"Sure, of course," Ellie answered as I was sitting within listening distance from the phone speaker.

"Ok, well they only went out three times, once to the movies, then to a car show and then to prom. Prom was the last date," Suzy lowered the volume in her voice almost to a whisper. I had to lean in to the phone receiver to hear better.

"Linda said that he was uneasy and weird to be around. I mean a nice guy, but not really interested in a lot of things. She said that he was preoccupied with fast cars and talked about running a Ferrari dealership one day," Suzy said.

"Anything else? Like did they make out and stuff?" Ellie asked openly. I covered my mouth to stifle any gasps.

"No, there was no chemistry. She even said he had bad breath and BO and that she should have stopped dating him after the first date. She also said he was just creepy."

"Did he ever talk about Kristen or his mom?" Ellie asked.

"Not that I know of, but she did mention that one day he would be rich and wouldn't have to worry about anything. Not sure what that meant, but maybe something about inheritance, I don't know?" said Suzy.

"Wow, what a weird guy. Hey, what was the guy's name who hung out with Alex at the student auto shop?" Ellie pried deeper. I clasped my hands in prayer.

"Geez, let's see, ahhhh.... Oh yeah, Barney 'butthead'. I can't remember his last name. OK then, I gotta get this English vocab done," said Suzy

"Sure, alright, talk to you later kiddo," Ellie hung up. Of course, I heard the conversation but listened to Ellie repeat most of the key information. Now, we needed to sift through some of the details.

Before dinner, I ran to Ernie's house. I could see him sitting in the kitchen doing some homework. I banged on the storm door and pressed my face against the glass.

"Hey, open up," I shouted. As I was making monkey faces at the door, Ernie's older brother, Frank patted me on the back.

"Hey, Chuckie, what's up man?" Frank announced. "Hey, I heard from Ernie that you guys are trying solve the murder thing with the Lundquist fam. If you need anything, let me know, OK?"

"Sure Frank, I will," I said with certainty. Frank opened the door. Ernie told me to sit down. Ernie chimed in.

"Hey, I overheard my folks talking last night."

"About what?" I said.

"There's something screwy going on with the Lundquists," said Ernie looking down at the note pad in front of him.

"You know my dad works for NS Insurance?"

"Yep." I nodded.

"He said that lots of people kill their family members to get life insurance money."

"That doesn't make sense. Why would the killer just kill Kristen?" I said.

"Ok, here's the latest. My mom briefly sat with Kristen's mom, after the visitation last night."

"What's that?" I asked.

"It's when people go see the dead body in a casket at the funeral home. To pay their respects."

"Geez I've never been to one," I said.

"Kids usually don't go, cause it scares the crap out of them," Ernie added.

"Have you been to a visitation?" I asked.

"Once. You know we're Catholics. Catholics like to drag their kids to funerals, do Rosaries and look at dead bodies and stuff. I went to my cousin Joey's wake, they call it that too. It was gross.

He hung himself. You could see the rope burn around his neck. The funeral guys tried to cover it up with makeup, but you could see it," Ernie grimaced.

"Jesus." I said.

"So, Kristen's mom said she, not Kristen was the target, and feels terribly guilty. She was supposed to go in the house with her, but dropped Kristen off first so that she could go to pick up some things from the store."

"Then that would make Alex the killer!" I spouted.

"Wrong, Alex reportedly has a solid alibi. He was at the high school auto shop. There are loads of witnesses," said Ernie.

"Who the hell besides Alex would kill them?" I said hunching over the table.

"There must have been a hit-man, someone hired to do the job. They messed up big time."

"What if Alex hired someone?" I said.

"Precisely, but who?"

"Time to do some work, and fast. Halloween is one week away," Ernie said.

Common sense would make sense here. We both thought of a prime suspect. Someone really dumb and stupid.

The next afternoon, the local news reported that a murder weapon had been found at the bottom of a pond in the Lundquist's backyard. It was a tire iron. That was a huge clue. The puzzle was coming together. Our plan to help the police needed to put into action. Ernie and I hatched a plan. A risky one. We needed Frank to help up out. He agreed.

That evening, I went back to Ernie's house. We asked Frank to join us to go over our plan. Ernie sat on his perfectly made bed. Frank and I sat on the floor littered with National Geographic and Mad magazines. His upstairs bedroom window was wide open to the cool Fall night. I started to complain.

"God, Ernie, make this fast, it's freezing in here," I quipped.

"Wimp," said Frank.

"Yeah, Wimp" said Ernie.

"I think Barney Shankles is our guy," Ernie announced.

"Yeah, I kinda think so too," I said.

"The guy is a turd. What kind of moron has B.S. as his initials?" Frank laughed, "he did it for his buddy Alex, and to make some cash on the side."

"That's what I think," said Ernie.

"I think you guys are on it, but how do we tell the cops?" I said.

"Here's the plan," Ernie said quietly. "We all have a pretty good idea that Barney did this. I think he was told by Alex to kill his mother. He killed Kristen instead then panicked and tossed the tire iron in the backyard pond. I'm sure that the cops are onto him, but we can speed this up."

"How so?" I said.

"Tell the cops, where the murder weapon came from." Ernie explained.

"Where did it come from?" I asked.

"Barney Butthead's trunk!" Frank said sarcastically.

"In every Dog Fart's trunk, you will find a tire iron and jack kit under the spare tire. You won't find one in Barney's Dog Fart!" Ernie elaborated.

"Alright, how do we prove this? Who's going to break into Shankles' trunk to see that the tire iron is missing?" I said.

"Chuck, you said earlier that Barney always drives down to the Forest Bakery on Saturday mornings and parks his Dog Fart in front. Right?" said Ernie.

"So what?"

"Well, if we can arrange for Barney to be stopped by the cops for driving with a flat tire, it's a whole new ballgame." Ernie smiled. "The cops would be notified of his crappy car driving to the bakery. They would be warned by us, ahead of time, that this is their suspect and that if they asked to help him change his flat tire, they would be able to confirm that there is no tire iron in the trunk, cause the detectives already have it," Ernie paused to catch his breath. "The end! The murderer is caught and Halloween is re-instated."

"Nice Ernie, but how does Butthead magically get a flat tire?" I asked.

"Sure, I knew that was your next question." Ernie chimed.

"This is where Frank comes in buddy boy," said Ernie presenting his hand toward Frank who was slouched against the bed frame. Frank scooted forward and pulled out a wicked looking tool from his windbreaker's side pocket.

"This, my friend Chuckie, is known as an awl. It has a dangerously sharp tip that is used to pierce tough materials, like thick leather, hardwoods and yes rubber too." Frank said assuredly. "If applied correctly to the carcass of a tire..."

"Wait, what? What's a tire carcass?" I asked.

"Sorry for using my mechanic talk," Frank chuckled. "The carcass of a tire is the wall of the tire, away from the thick tread. It's thin and the weakest part of a tire. Comprende?"

"Ok but ah, who is going to jab that thing into Barney's tire?" I knew what was coming.

"It's logistics, Chuck," said Ernie. "You are by far the smallest and thinnest of all of us. It only makes sense that you are the guy for the job." Ernie looked right at me and raised his eyebrows.

"What the Hell!"

"Me?"

"Why me?" I whined.

"I told you why. It's really not a big deal. You're doing this not only to capture a killer, but you'll spare Halloween for all the kids in Forest Bluff. That's something to think about." Ernie said emphatically.

"All you need to do is slide under Barney's Dog Fart tomorrow night. Stick the awl into the sidewall of one of the rear tires. Once the awl pierces the rubber, you just carefully push the awl all the way in, until it goes no further." Frank demonstrated this procedure with a piece of scrap paper, pushing the sharp awl through the sheet of paper.

"So, isn't the damn thing going to pop, blow up or something?" I said.

"No, it shouldn't make any noise. The pressure around the awl shaft won't allow it to leak," Frank confirmed. I wanted to call off the whole thing, but duty demanded otherwise.

"So, how is the tire going to get flat?" I asked.

"Well, as long as the car doesn't move the punctured tire will remain intact. But when Mr. Butthead heads out to the bakery the next morning, centrifugal force will spin the awl out of the tire and *voila*, the Dog Fart's tire goes flat," Frank said factually, then crossed his arms confidently.

"Ok, who is going to call the cops and when?" I said.

"Either Ellie or me, but we have to deliver an anonymous note to Chief Dunn tomorrow afternoon, for a heads up," Ernie said.

"Anonymous note?" I asked. "And who's is going to write that?"

"I will," said Ernie. "Then we'll ask Ellie to drop it off at the station."

"What if this plan fails? I said.

"Then it fails. Barney gets caught later and Halloween is toast," Ernie sighed.

We all looked at each other and there was a moment of thought.

"Ok, let's do it," I said, feeling a bit like James Bond accepting a daring mission.

"Perfect," said Ernie. Frank got up and handed me the awl.

"Don't cut yourself with that thing."

"I won't," I said as I gripped the awl's pointed end like a kid taught to hold scissors.

"I'll start writing the note to Chief Dunn," Ernie reported. "Then give it to Ellie to drop it off."

"I'll scope out Barney's driveway tomorrow," I said.

The plan was in motion. The next morning, I got the note for Chief Dunn. I gave it to Ellie after school. The envelope was addressed; '*To Chief Dunn, Very Important! Please read. Thank you.*'

Before the envelope was sealed. I opened the handwritten note and read it:

Dear Chief Dunn,

We need your help.

1967 forest green Dodge Dart with flat tire driving from Scott

Street to Forest Bakery at 7am this coming Saturday.

Be on the look-out.

This guy is probably someone you are looking for.

Check His trunk.

The police have something that belonged to him.

"Why do I have to drop this letter off?" Ellie complained.

"Cause, you are a cute girl and the office won't suspect anything. They'll think that you're giving the Chief a thank you note or a drawing from art class or something like that," I grinned.

"Ok then, I'll take it there on my way to the rec center," Ellie said as she took the envelope with the message inside.

Ellie was in 10th grade, three years ahead of me. Her determination for truth and justice were defined by the lingering Vietnam war, anti-pollution and women's rights issues. Her strong opinions took many by surprise, due to her small frame, and charming presence. We were lucky to have her on our team. Ellie worked several hours a week at the recreation center downtown. She did menial office work but was enthusiastic about her duties. Ellie dropped off the note to Chief Dunn. Everything was going as planned. It was Friday afternoon. The tire puncture mission was nearing. It would happen after sundown. Going to school was a waste, I couldn't think of anything else except crawling under Barney's car in the dark.

At least it wasn't raining. I carefully selected my clothes to wear. Dark pants, shirt and crappy old brown jacket. I ran over to Ernie's house to tell him to follow me over to Scott Street. We both hopped on our bikes and headed out in the darkness.

"You got the awl?" Ernie asked.

"Yep, right here," I said while feeling the outline of the awl's bulb like handle in my jacket pocket. Ernie handed me a mini flash light.

"You're gonna need this," he said very seriously. I took the flash light and stuffed it in my front pocket.

"Ok, let's go," I said quietly.

The night was cold and crisp. The smell of the fallen leaves tried to distract me. Since I thought that I might be dead soon, life and everything around me was so good. I kept telling myself that soon this will be over.

As we got to the edge of Noble Ave. and Scott Street, Ernie and I slowed to a stop. It was really dark. That was good, but finding Shankles' driveway was difficult.

"Ok, there it is, in the driveway," Ernie whispered.

"I see it," I said. The Dog Fart was parked right at the edge of the sidewalk and the driveway. Ernie stayed back as a look out one house back. I set my bike against an oak tree. As I got closer to the car I could see the flickering of a television through the drawn porch blinds of the old frame house where Barney lived. I could hear muffled yelling coming from inside. Barney lived with his mother, who drank a lot. I walked closer to the parked car, making sure not to be seen. After quickly looking both ways and checking to see if Ernie was watching, he gave me a thumbs up. I snapped my head back to focus on the car. My heart was pounding. I knelt behind the car's trunk and wiggled on my stomach to wedge myself between the two rear tires. I was a skinny and compact kid. Ernie was right, neither him nor Frank could have done this. I could still hear Barney's mom barking out orders of some sort. The television got louder. I reached into my jacket pocket to pull out the awl.

"No problem," I mumbled.

I then awkwardly attempted to wrangle the flashlight in my front pocket. It was in my jeans front pocket. I couldn't get it out. Lying on my stomach made it next to impossible.

"Damn it," I winced. Scraping the top of my right hand on the pavement.

"Goddamn it," I said to myself. It was a bitch trying to get the light out, but in desperation, I did it. I flicked on the mini light to locate the tire wall. I tightly squeezed the awl's handle and made the decision for point of entry. I pin-pointed the spot and while juggling the flashlight with my left hand and grasping the awl handle with my right, I began to apply pressure to the tire wall. Up to now, all was good. I quickly peeked under the car and could see Ernie's feet and bike tires. I resumed my vandalism.

"What the hell in taking so long!" yelled Barney's mom. I could hear the porch door fly open. I froze, shut off the light and held my breath.

"Jesus mom, I'll be there in a minute," Barney yelled back. I could hear his clumsy footsteps coming down the front porch stairs and the storm door slamming. I saw his Dingo boots as he sat on the stoop of the stairs. I heard him light up a cigarette. Toss the match near the driveway lip. I caught a whiff of the tobacco. I froze.

"Hey you," Barney barked. I almost wet myself. I remained still.

"Hey you little bastard," Barney yelled.

"Me?" Ernie squeaked.

"Yeah, You! Who else would I be talking to?" Barney said sarcastically.

I could hear Ernie jump on the bike seat and smash his feet on the petals. Ernie left me alone. Alone to die! As I prepared for the worst, I kept quiet and still.

"Damn it Barney, where in the hell is my booze?" his mother demanded.

"What a bitch," Barney mumbled loudly to himself. I could hear him step up to the door. He opened it.

"Listen, I'll get your drink in a couple," Barney said.

I could hear the door close, but again, Barney came down the porch stairs. He paused and walked up to the driver's side of the Dodge. His dirty boots were just inches from my face. I held my breath. This was it, I thought.

My mind went into a tailspin. My Lutheran guilt kicked in. If only I had not ditched confirmation classes last month, this wouldn't be happening, I thought. God's punishment! Then Barney shuffled his boots on the driveway and stepped to the front end of the car. I heard him wrestling with his pants. I heard what sounded like a zipper. My hands pressed against the rear driver's side tire and both feet jammed to the tire wheel on the other side. I got another nose full of cigarette smoke, but the worst was yet to come. Barney began to relieve himself as he leaned back on the hood of his car. Like most driveways, this one inclined toward the street. In a matter of seconds, I would be swimming in Barney's piss. I wanted to cry. He peed for what seemed like fifteen minutes. The splattering sound ended as I could begin to feel the warm pee cozy up like a beaver damn against my shirt and pants. I heard him zip up and head back up the porch steps and slam the door shut. I was disgusted with my predicament. No time to complain. Stick the damn awl into the tire and get the hell out of here I thought. Frank didn't tell me how hard piercing tire walls could be. Once I could feel the tip of the awl in, the air pressure was limiting the penetration. After a few cussing-prayers, I jammed the entire awl shaft all the way in. Praise the Lord!

"Shit," I whispered. As I wiggled and sloshed out from under the car. I extended my head up and outward like a turtle so my face wouldn't touch Barney's pee. I scrambled up, stuffed the flash light in my jeans and ran to my bike. I quickly glanced back to check out the crime scene. I rode home with wet clothing and the stench of Barney's urine. Although wet and cold, I couldn't have felt prouder of myself.

Before I entered the house, I stripped off my pee soaked clothing and pitched them in the outside trash. In my damp underwear, I bolted up to the upstairs bathroom. I chucked my undies in the waste can, took a hot shower, with lots of soap and headed to bed. I was mad at Ernie for leaving me there alone, but after thinking about it, I would've done the same.

I looked out my bedroom window and could see Ernie peering out his window. I waved to get his attention. He looked back at me and shrugged his shoulders. I gave him a thumb up. He returned the gesture and then raised six fingers. I nodded my head and saluted. Ernie and I set our alarm clocks to 6am.

I woke up before the alarm sounded. Threw on my clean jeans and a sweatshirt. Ran down stairs and scarfed down an untoasted Pop-Tart, chugged some milk from the carton and rode over to Ernie's house. He was heading out the back door as I pulled up on my bike.

"Man, I thought he was gonna kill you," Ernie sighed. "Jesus!"

"Yeah, I kinda felt the same when you took off like a weenie," I said.

"Sorry, I had no choice." said Ernie.

"You won't believe what Old Butthead did after you left?" I said.

"What?" said Ernie.

"Well, just before I jammed the awl in the tire, he took a leak," I reported.

"On you!" Ernie blurted.

"No, he pissed on the driveway and it flowed under the car. I got soaked."

"Oh man," Ernie laughed.

"Sure, go ahead dickhead, laugh!" I said emphatically. Then we both laughed at the grossness of it all.

"Time to stake out the bakery," said Ernie.

"I hope Frank's idea works?" I spouted.

"Yep, me too," said Ernie.

So off we rode to the Forest Bakery. We both put on our wool hats. The sun was coming up and the chill in the air was refreshing. Within five minutes we pulled around Illinois Road on to Western Avenue. The Bakery was just near the main intersection in the center of town. We pulled over near the Village Drug store. We had a good view and were at a safe distance. The streets were quiet, no cars were parked in front of the bakery. We waited, and waited. There was no sign of Barney's Dodge.

"Damn it," Ernie said, "Where is he? You said that he shows up like clockwork," Ernie said mockingly, like a toddler.

"He does!" I said sharply. "What if the tire blew out last night in the driveway, or maybe on his way here?"

"Wait, wait, do you see that? Can you hear that sound?" I said.

"It's the Dog Fart from Hell!"

"Oh Christ," Ernie mumbled. We watched in awe as Barney approached the curbside lot in front of the bakery. His head was sticking out the window, looking back at the rear of the car. The car was listing to the rear left while making a loud clattering with every revolution of the rear tire.

Barney maneuvered the wounded car to his favorite spot. He looked out the window and twisted his head as far back as he could to see what was wrong with his car. He looked really pissed. The door flew open. He bolted out to see the deflating tire. He quickly dropped to his knees, then on to his stomach. We could see Barney's legs precariously sticking out into the road. As he was fiddling around underneath his car, the owner from the Surprise Shop, a toy store next to the bakery, peeked out the door, then closed it. You could hear Barney cussing and banging on the bumper. Ernie and I walked our bikes across the street near the train depot and closer to the action. We could see Barney wiggling, kicking his legs and swearing like a sailor. This was a show worth seeing in spite of the risks.

"Holy crap!" I yelped. A deafening ear-piercing balloon-like squeak could be heard within blocks of the bakery. Just then, a Forest Bluff squad car pulled up behind Barney's car. Barney rolled out from under the car, holding the awl in his hand. Alarmed by seeing the squad car, he twisted his neck to get a better look and smacked his forehead into the bumper. The Officer stepped out of the squad car and walked to the rear end of the Dog Fart, glared down at Barney, lying on the pavement with the awl in his right hand and legs sprawled outwards like Leonardo Da Vinci's drawing *The Vitruvian Man.* The Officer placed his hands on his service belt. We listened intensely, but pretended to be fixing our bike chains.

"So, what ya doing?" The Officer asked.

"Nothing," said Barney, being snarky.

"Well, it looks like something," said the Officer "What's the awl for?"

"It was in my tire. Can't you see it's flat?" Barney spouted.

"Oh yeah, I see it's flat alright," said the officer.

"Look, it's my car," said Barney.

"I need to see your driver's license."

"Sure, give me second," said Barney as he dropped the awl and wrangled the bulging black wallet from his back pocket. Just as Barney handed the license to the Officer, another squad car pulled up next to the Dog Fart and parked right in front of the car's front end. Ernie and I had front row seats.

"Holy crap, it's Chief Dunn," I said under my breath.

"He must've read my letter." Ernie said excitedly. The Officer nodded to Chief Dunn. They quietly conferred with each other for a moment while looking at Barney's license. Ernie and I, as well as a growing pool of onlookers, could hear what the officers were discussing.

"Mr. Shankles?" The Officer questioned.

"Yep, that's me," Barney smirked.

"We need to see your vehicle registration," Chief Dunn said in a calm low voice.

"Ah, ok, let's see, it should be in the glove compartment," Barney said.

"Want me to get it?

"No, you stay put. We'll get it," said Chief Dunn. The other Officer reached in to the interior and after a couple minutes came out empty handed.

"No registration in the glove compartment," said the Officer.

"Oh, it might be in the...trunk?" Barney said anxiously.

"You got the key?" asked Chief Dunn.

"Yeah sure, ah, it's in the ignition," said Barney still sitting on the pavement. Chief Dunn took the keys out of the car and walked around to open the trunk. Ernie and I were like big time gamblers watching the last lengths of a horse race with an 10/1 payoff. Chief Dunn handed the keys to the other officer, who then opened the trunk. Chief Dunn at first stood back to survey the contents, he then could be seen poking at something with his nightstick. He paused for a moment, then pointed to something. We couldn't see what the officers were staring at. Suddenly, Barney leaped to his feet, high-tailing it to the other side of the train tracks. He whipped right by us. Ernie and I winced. The Chief bolted into the squad car, while the Officer pursued Barney on foot. We hopped on our bikes and followed the foot chase now passing the Forest Bluff library and heading into the city park. We were just a few yards away from Barney. He looked back at us. Geez, watching Barney run with his shit-kicking Dingo boots was a sight to behold. Ernie and I were now ahead of the Officer.

"You little bastards," Barney said gasping for air, "I'm gonna kill you too!"

The officers heard what he said, just as Ernie drove next to Barney and twisted his handlebars in Barney's path. Ernie flew off the bike hitting his butt on the turf. The Officer lunged. It was a stunning tackle. Barney hit the ground hard. I peeled off to the left just missing Barney's head. Chief Dunn pulled the Squad car into the park. Two more officers arrived at the edge of the park. The chase had ended. Barney was in handcuffs. I rode my bike over to check on Ernie.

"You alright?" I said.

"Jesus, my freaking ass. I fell right on my ass!" Ernie whined.

"Yeah, but it was worth it." I said with a big smile. We both looked at one another. I helped Ernie off the ground.

"You know, we did something good today," I said.

"Yeah, the cops wanted Barney, we just helped," Ernie said.

"I'll bet they saw the missing tire iron in the trunk?" I said.

"Yeah and maybe something else?" Ernie suggested.

The cops did find something else, a stained handkerchief with Kristen's blood on it. The following day it was reported on the headline of the local paper:

Lundquist Murderers Caught! Brother of Victim Confesses to Hiring Friend as Hit-Man!

"I can't believe this!" Ellie cried, "How could her own brother do something like this?"

"It's sick," Ernie replied, as he gently placed his hand on Ellie's shoulder.

"It's not just sick, but totally insane," I added. "Did you read stuff about why they did it?"

"For money, money to buy fast cars and then sell them overseas for big bucks," Ernie said.

"What a bunch of morons," I said.

"So senseless, poor Kristen," Ellie said tearfully.

"At least they were caught," Ernie declared.

"Yeah, thank God for that!" I said.

The town of Forest Bluff was relieved by the killer's capture. Two days following the apprehension, Mayor Grant announced that city would resume Halloween. Most parents welcomed this. They wanted their kids to have some sort of normalcy. Some residents did darken their homes. In our neighborhood, life went on. Ernie was supposed to be an astronaut. He looked like a pudgy John Glenn wearing a Japanese pearl diving mask. My costume resembled something between Count Dracula and Astro Boy. People handing out candy kept asking me what I was supposed to be. I told them I was the son Eddie from the 'Munster's' TV show. It worked! I got bonus handouts.

After about two hours of trick and treating, Ernie and I came back home. Ernie followed me up to my bedroom where we dumped the goods out in two separate piles. We separated the candies we liked from the ones that could be donated to siblings. Butter Fingers, Baby Ruth, Mounds and Pay Day candy bars were golden. O'Henrys , Almond Joy, and Dots were tolerable but not worthy of our refined taste buds. Ellie knocked on the door.

"Hey, can I come in?" She asked.

"Sure," I said.

"So, did you guys get a lot of stuff?" Ellie queried, while eyeing the hills of candies on the bed.

"Yup, gotta lot of goodies," said Ernie.

"Oh, I love O'Henrys," Ellie sparkled.

"They're all yours kiddo," I said pointing to the pile of misfit candies.

"Gee, thanks," Ellie said while scooping up the pile. Frank walked into the room. He saw Ellie holding a handful of chocolate bars.

"Happy Halloween everyone!" Frank shouted. "I just wanted to check up on you kids. Your mom let me know that you were upstairs and invited me in," Frank said.

"Where's your costume?" Ellie asked.

"Nope, I'm too old for that!" Frank said laughing.

"But I'm not too old to help you guys inspect your loot." He added.

"Sure, help yourself," I said.

"You can have some of my candy when we get home," Ernie said. Frank snapped a Baby Ruth from my pile. As he munched on the bar, a cold breeze blew from my bedroom window. We all sat quietly listening to Frank chewing and crinkling the candy wrapper in his hand. That Halloween night in 1971 was a life changing passage. Murder put Forest Bluff on the front page. The need to mourn our classmate was heavy on our minds. Us kids had to improvise. The cold wind blew stronger. We sat in silence, picking at our piles of candy.

Ellie became a journalist for a cable news network, sometimes she calls me when she's not busy. Ernie went to law school and became a district attorney for the City of Minneapolis. Sadly, Ernie's brother Frank died in motorcycle accident shortly after his twenty-fifth birthday, one day before Halloween. Barney Shankles is serving a life sentence in federal prison. Alex Lundquist committed suicide while awaiting his trial. The rest of us will never forget Kristen and the Halloween that might not have been.

Bus Ride

Us kids were messing around on the slushy sidewalk at our bus stop. The neighbor's filthy English Sheep dog ran zig-zag in between us standing in line. I hated that dog. It was aggressive and had a nasty fruit basket that dangled under its dirty matted hair.

"Buzz off Puff," said one of the kids.

"Get your dirty nuts outta here!" yelled another as the dog smeared his jacket with mud. This was just the pre-show for the daily bus ride. Our stop was last. The bus route was overcrowded with high school teens from the Southeast side of Forest Bluff. We had our fair share of bullies on the bus. The town knew about these kids and their hooliganism. Us kids just wanted to avoid them. We waited to hear the sound of the bus winding around the road. We hoped that some of the earlier pick-ups either missed the ride, or called in sick. The better chances of finding a seat, especially closer to the front. No one wanted to sit in the back of the bus.

"It's coming," shouted a trio of anxious riders. The bus, crusted with dirty black snow and icicles on the rims slowly pulled up to the stop sign. The girls in the group got on first. I was last, and anxious. The bi-fold door opened, the heated bus reeked of bologna sandwiches, banana, vomit and freshly melted snow. One by one we stepped up hauling our school packs and lunch buckets. Frantically searching the sea of bobbing heads for an open seat, all while attempting to look cool. Nerdy shrimps like me with thick glasses were open game. I could see that all the seats in front of me were taken, except in the very back.

"Ok, find a seat," said Mr. Oliver, our bus driver. He pulled the lever back to close the door. "There are seats in the back," he said looking at me through the long rearview mirror. Yeah, like I didn't know that? Jesus Lord, my stomach cringed. There he was, Big Johnny, king of the shitheads, staring right at me from the last seat, legs spread-eagle in dirty jeans. His greasy black hair divided hard in the middle, he eyed me like a buzzard would a fresh roadkill. He lifted his middle finger with his right hand resting on his knee, and grinned exposing his slimy green teeth.

"Hey Burnsie, we got plenty of room back here," he chuckled. It was Big Johnny Holster and his troupe of hyenas. The bus started moving. I was in panic mode. Big Johnny stood up and began to walk towards me leaning from side to side holding on to the isles seat backs to keep his tall lanky body upright. I swallowed hard. He came forward and lowered his ugly mug right in my face. I focused on the blackheads around his nose.

"Hey, didn't ya here me Burnsie," Big Johnny said. I listened.

"We, have plenty of room in the back," unloading his onion laced cigarette breath into my face.

"Sure, ah ok," I squeaked. Suddenly, I felt a light touch on my jacket.

"Charlie, you can sit next to me," said a soft voice. It was Aida. She was a student at my Mom's ballet school and good friend of my older sister.

"Oh hi," I said. "Thanks." Big Johnny couldn't believe that his meal had been snatched by a gorgeous senior. He was pissed. Aida scooted against the window. I was grateful. I knew that Johnny would somehow get me back for this *pie in the face* embarrassment, but for now all I cared about was a bus ride to school.

My day began in Western Civilization. Mr. Occhipinni's class was fun. A tough Chicago Italian that made learning fun. Physical Education was my second class of the day. We had wrestling instruction and practice in the main gym. I wasn't motivated. There was nothing more gross to me than flopping around on a mat with another guy, grunting, groaning, sweating and drooling. The object was to pin your opponent on his back with both shoulders touching the mat. Our PE Coach picked out two guys from the wrestling team to demonstrate technique. The Coach then divided us into pairs according to weight and height. I was the smallest freshman in the class. I got paired with a short stocky kid I once knew from junior high.

"Hey Max," I said.

"Hi Chuckster," said Max. My nickname in eighth grade.

"Ok boys," said the Coach, "assume your positions." That meant one of us had to get on all fours, like a dog, and the other guy on his knees crouched over the opponent's back with one arm around the waist. Then Coach's whistle would blow and the fun began. I was the top opponent and could barely get my arm around Max's doughy waist. I had to wear an elastic band to hold my thick glasses on.

"Ready?" said Coach. I could smell that Max hadn't bathed for a while. I didn't want to hold him like we were told.

"Go!" said Coach tooting the whistle. Max didn't waste time. He took advantage of his weight and threw me back. I hit the mat and he flipped over before I could think.

"Gotcha!" Max shouted. He had me pinned, both shoulders to the mat. I had been fooled by this chubby dude. I was mad. We both looked at the Coach. Other guys pinned their partner in seconds, and others tossed about until the Coach blew the time out whistle.

"Ok boys, change positions," said Coach. Great, now I had to get on all fours. Max was good at this. He grabbed me really tight and had the advantage of being on top. I had a caveman moment. I wanted to show who's the man here? The starter whistle blew. Max did his best to push me over. I resisted, then let him try again. This time I didn't fight. Max pushed so hard that he rolled like a turtle on to his back. I twisted around and leapt onto his chest pinning both shoulders.

"Jesus Chuckster!" Max yelped.

"AHHHHHH," I belted. "Had enough?" I hadn't felt this kind of violent rush before. Coach had us change partners a couple times. I outwitted them all. Coach looked at me and was impressed. There was a flash of a moment where I thought, "Hey PE is OK." The smell of the locker room killed that thought. I ate a forgettable lunch before English lit then had to endure a lecture on STDs in Health Management. Gas and a sore throat became my biggest problem while our health teacher was reviewing the ravages of syphilis and gonorrhea; good to know!

My last class of the day was algebra. I felt a cold coming on. I had a lot of mucus irritating my throat. I was coughing a lot. It sounded like a smoker's hack. Maybe I caught something when Big Johnny breathed in my face? I sounded horrible. Kids avoided me in the hallway. I walked into the classroom and plopped down in my seat. Sitting in front of me was Big Johnny's younger brother Keith Holster. He hated my guts. He called me four eyes, and pizza face. His face was flat, had grey teeth, and shark eyes. I did envy Keith's thick well- groomed hair, it was perfect, not like his brother Johnny's. I hacked again into my hand. I tried to keep quiet. The cough wouldn't stop. I started to sound like a seal. I didn't want to piss off Keith. He held grudges about everything.

"Alright, today we'll review our assignments from last Friday," said Ms. Almond. While we were all looking for our papers, a chunk of phlegm fell back into my throat. I had a gag reflex and coughed hard. I felt better. I could breathe again. God, it felt good to breathe. The damn tickling in my throat was gone. Thank God, no more gagging. I found my Algebra homework from Friday. I looked it over.

"Now, before we review, make sure you have both pages," Ms. Almond said. As I looked up at the chalk board, I adjusted my glasses and saw something that terrified me. Ms. Almond's voice didn't register anymore. I went blank for a moment, then broke out into a cold sweat. I was having an out of body experience. Reality snapped back when the girl next to me dropped her book on the floor. I reached down to pick it up for her hoping that my eyes were playing tricks on me. No, the eyes weren't kidding. There it was, clinging to Keith's dew. A large chunk of green mucus, stuck perfectly to the back of his head. It was mine. I made it and I spewed the throat snot. It was apparent that Keith had no idea this slimy blob was hanging from his amazing hair. I pretended to get something out of my backpack under the desk chair. I scanned the faces of the kids sitting next to me to look for any abnormal expressions; None!

"Hot damn," I thought out loud. "There is a God." I looked at the wall clock. Only ten minutes left of class. I thought of excusing myself from class, but this would surely implicate me. I wanted to get out before Keith took out his comb. Ms. Almond handed out our new assignments. I had no idea what she was saying. I just glared at the clump of goop in front of me. I planned my exit from the class as soon as the hour bell rang. How he would find the slime chunk, not my problem. He had a lot of enemies. Anyone one of them could have hawk spitted on his head. It could be mistaken for bird shit? I thought.

"Class is dismissed," Ms. Almond said. Before I even had a chance to get up, Keith grabbed his backpack and took off. No one noticed his phlegmy ornament. I was relieved. I picked up my stuff and headed to my locker. I thought about the moment he would fix his hair and come across my masterpiece mucus blob. I had a good laugh.

Thursday's bus ride to school was terrific. Most of the delinquents including Big Johnny were ditching class. There were plenty of seats. Even the bus cabin stench was tolerable. It was going to be a great day.

"Alright, today we're doing something fun. We will have a mixed class wrestling competition. This class will wrestle the class next door." Coach said. We were all trying to think what guys were in that class. Some of us ran over to the metal door dividing the gyms and peeked through the small mesh glass window.

"Oh damn," one of the guys said. "Big Johnny's in that class."

"Wait," I said, "He wasn't on the morning bus?"

"Sometimes he gets a ride," said a neighborhood kid.

"I thought that class was only for freshmen?" I said.

"No, if you failed PE as a freshman you gotta retake it as a sophomore. Holster failed last year," said Max. We all got quiet. The thought of having to wrestle Big Johnny was bad news.

"Tough cheese for the dude who gets to pair with Holster," Max said.

"Yep, so true," I said.

"Better take your vitamins," said Max.

"Too late." I said.

Coach opened the door and told the class in the adjacent room to come in for the wrestling session. I tried to make myself disappear in the crowd of white T-shirts and blue shorts. There were two other guys with glasses, but I stood out like a fly in buttermilk, being the smallest guy at Forest Bluff High.

"Alright, I'm going to pair you boys off with opponents from the other class," Coach said. He made us stand in two lines on opposite sides of the mats. Our line was like a stock market chart, high and low. The opponents line was all one height. This made it easy for Coach. He simply glanced down at his clipboard.

"Ok, your wrestling buddy will be the guy standing across from you." Each class looked up and acknowledged their opponent. I was cleaning off my thick glasses and adjusted the elastic frame strap to the back of my head. I looked up to see who I was going to battle. This was not what I had expected. There had to be some mistake in Coach's pairing.

"Hey Burnsie," said Big Johnny. His sardine breath in my face.

"This is going to be fun," He smiled.

"Hey Big Johnny," I mumbled.

"So, is that chick on the bus your friend or what?" said Big Johnny.

"Yup," I said. Coach motioned everyone to find places on the mats to begin our wrestling.

"Boys, we are going to have two pairs wrestling at the same time," Coach said. "This way, we can all watch how each pair uses their technique." He pointed at four guys standing in the center of the mats.

"You guys are first," Coach said. He tapped the shoulders of the kids who had to be on all fours first. One pair was Max and this bean pole guy.

"Wrestle," said Coach, blowing his whistle. We watched and rooted for our classmates. I saw Max use his belly weight move to throw off the bean pole. It was like watching a scarecrow get pounced by a pig runt. Max won both times. I looked behind me and Big Johnny was adjusting his gym shorts. You could see that he wasn't wearing a jock strap. He wore his loose boxer briefs instead. Jesus, I couldn't believe this was going to happen.

"Burns, Holster, you're next," said Coach. He picked another pair across from us. We took our positions as instructed. I was on top of Big Johnny first. When he was on all fours, I had to raise my knee off the mat in order to even put my arm around him. Here I was hugging my bus stop bully. This was so damn messed up.

"You do one weird thing, Burnsie, and you're a dead man!" Big Johnny said. I didn't say a word. I looked up at Coach and he took his whistle hanging from his neck. My mind was churning. Should I just let him win? No. Should I ...

"Wrestle," said Coach.

"Your momma teaches ballet. Can I call you Twinkle-toes?" Big Johnny whispered. I hated when I was called that. I held tighter.

"You're getting weird," he said. I braced myself and tried to push him over. He didn't budge. He laughed as I fell on my ass.

"Alright Twinkle-toes." I rolled on my stomach to prevent an easy pin. Big Johnny grabbed my waist and rolled me like a burrito on my back. I pushed to stop him from crushing my chest. He thrust his hairy arms down to stick my shoulders to the mat. Big Johnny held me down.

"That's it Twinkle-toes." He rose up and raised his arms in victory. I laid on the mat staring at the ceiling's steel I-beams. It wasn't over.

"Ok boys, change positions," said Coach. We did. I knew that Big Johnny had the advantage now. He was in the drivers' seat. I was screwed. How could this change? "Jesus Christ," I screamed silently. Now in my dog pose, I looked over to Coach. He smiled at me a gave me a nod of hope. I looked toward the door to the cafeteria, lovely

Aida was leaning against the wall. She saw me and waved. This was a different ball game. This was a face-off with destiny.

"Ready boys?" Coach asked. He could see that everyone in class was watching us. The other pair of wrestlers could only see the backs of their classmates. In my dog position, Big Johnny painfully yanked his arm tightly around my waist. He breathed heavy close to my head. Wafts of tobacco, fish and bologna scented air filled my nose. I had no strategy, just revenge for this asshole.

"Wrestle," Coach yelled. He was excited too.

"Twinkle-toes, you're toast!" yelled Johnny. Everyone could hear it.

I pushed the bastard up so he lost his grip. Johnny flew onto his back. I fell onto his stomach. My face was buried in his furry arm-pit.

"Shit," Johnny yelled. As I wiggled out from his grasp, my elbow caught the waistband of his shorts. Coach almost blew his whistle to end the match. By the time I got back on my knees to attack, Johnny's junk was in full view. Now, the class became English rugby fans. Coach fell back behind the fans.

"Fight, fight, fight, fight...." The crowd yelled. It was a shot of adrenaline. To hell with technique. I jumped on Johnny's hairy belly and pinned his shoulders to the mat.

"Goddam you Burns," Big Johnny shouted. He reached up and ripped my glasses off. This was the last straw. I was a blind, angry, and mad little son of a bitch. The cheering fans got louder.

"Fight, fight, fight...." I got angrier. I began to punch and pound Johnny's upper body and head relentlessly. Johnny tried to kick me like a baby.

"Fight, fight, fight...." Turned into, "Burns, Burns, Burns, Burns...." I was loving it. I couldn't see a thing but could smell blood from Big Johnny's greasy nose. The chanting of my name was freaking amazing. I was the center of attention. I was the dragon slayer. The crowd were my people. Humiliation had been defeated; for me at least. Coach blew the whistle.

"Ok, match over," said Coach. Big Johnny laid on the mat nursing his shame. Aida had gone to pick up my glasses and handed them to me. I quickly put them on. I didn't want to miss any of this.

"Nice job Charlie," she said smiling.

"Thanks," I said. The entertainment was over. My classmates would spread the news of my victory. I was in a good place. Johnny's brother Keith stopped calling me four-eyes and pizza face. Not sure if he ever found that giant bugger on his head. Bus rides became tolerable from now on, but I preferred to ride my bike to school anyhow, even in the snow.

Dance Belt Required

"Come on boys, jump higher," yelled Ms. Ruth. Gary and I loved being noticed in class. The girls would whisper behind us telling Gary and me how to do the steps. We couldn't get enough of this attention. Ballet class was the best!

"That's more like it. Jump second and first, repeat close fifth," said Ms. Ruth. I was the last kid in the class to learn the combinations. And, just when I learned it, she would change the combination.

"Chuck, don't worry. You'll get it," she would say. Gary would snicker as well as some of the advanced dancers stretching on the floor before the next class. I smiled and joked with them all. This only made me work harder. Gary and I were in the elementary level ballet class. We were both close to fourteen. Being boys in ballet was not always easy. Lots of peer pressure, teasing and bullying. Gary and I kept our afterschool dance classes kind of a secret. Kids knew about it but since my mom owned the Dance Centre, they didn't hassle me too much. Gary would just punch the crap out of any prick who made fun of him. Every Tuesday and Thursday afternoon we would go to dance classes. It was great! Gorgeous girls all spiffed up with their hair in buns. The smell of sweat and leather slippers; it was pure heaven for two guys who were fascinated with girls and athleticism.

As a little kid, my parents couldn't stop me from dancing around the house. Music was always playing. They encouraged me and watched me perform. Give me a striped blazer from the rummage shop, play "Music Man's" *Seventy-Six Trombones on the record player*, and you've got a show! I learned all sorts of men's dance steps from some of my Mother's colleagues. Russian sit-kicks, coffee grinders, and split jumps were my favorites. I started taking ballet when I was seven. I was the only boy in class. I was shy, but this was a nice place to be. Gary started taking classes a few years later. His dad was an M.D. and believed that classical ballet was an excellent cross-training activity. Gary could've cared less about cross-training for downhill skiing, he enjoyed the scenery, talking, flirting and showing off to the chatty girls.

In late September, Ms. Ruth approached Gary and me about an opportunity to perform. Boys were in demand. It was for a local dance company's Nutcracker ballet. We both said yes.

"This will be a great experience for you boys," Ms. Ruth said.

"I'll get the schedule and rehearsal information sheets to your parents. The rehearsals start in two weeks." Gary and I were excited. We didn't even have to audition. Ms. Ruth and my Mom recommended us. The following week, we both got welcome letters from the Lake Side Ballet Company director:

Dear Charles Burns,

Here are the rehearsal information sheets and schedules for the LSBC's production of the "Nutcracker" ballet. Please read all the information carefully. Rehearsal attire for *boys: Black tights, white t-shirts, white sox, black canvas ballet slippers. Dance Belts Required!*

See you soon,

Marvin Viscount, Ballet Master LSBC

After reading this, I picked up the phone to call Gary.

"Hello, hey, what the hell is a dance belt?" Gary asked.

"I thought you knew?" I asked.

"Did you ask your mom? She'd know," Gary said.

"She said that it's something men dancers need to wear. When they get older and more advanced."

"What?" Gary said

"She said the dance wear store will show me. I'm going this Saturday to buy the stuff we need. Want to go?"

"Sure, what time?"

"We'll need to take the train downtown," I said.

"Ok," said Gary.

"The store is on Wabash near the Palmer House. How about nine o'clock?

"Perfect," said Gary.

"Later man," I said.

We walked from Madison Avenue to Wabash Street. The dance store was in one of the old tall office buildings on the seventh floor. Stepping out of the elevator we knew we were in the right place. The smell of leather and spandex garments filled the lobby. Kids were trying on ballet slippers, tap and pointe shoes while some parents sat and watched. Gary and I looked around the room for a sign or a display for men's dance wear.

"Can I help you boys?" asked one of the sales ladies.

"Yes. We were wondering if you sell dance belts for boys...ah, or men?" Gary asked.

"Of course, what style and color?" she asked.

"Ah," Gary stumbled.

"Could you show us what they look like?" I said sheepishly.

"Sure, one moment," the sales lady said. She went to the stock room.

"Why don't they put these dance belts out on display?" Gary said.

"Yeah, what's the deal here?" I said. The lady came back with several small boxes. She set them on the sales desk.

"What size waist are you?" She said. I was trying to imagine what was in the boxes she brought out. Gary was looking at the boxes too.

"Small or Medium? These are for you guys, right?" She asked.

"Ah, yeah for us," I said. She then opened a box labeled Small/Nude. Both Gary and I watched the lady pull out the small garment. We thought that she had brought out the wrong boxes. These did not look like belts! Of course, we didn't know what to expect. I didn't see any buckles. She then shook the garment and stretched it out so we could see it better.

"Nice, aren't they? The nude color is best for any kind of tights," She said, while turning the slinky modified jock-strap in different angles. Gary and I had always worn dance trunks or just plain underwear under our loose fitting elementary dance shorts. This was a shock! These things looked like some kind of weirdo sex panties.

"So, is this what you were looking for?" asked the sales lady.

"Ah, ah, yes, I think? Are all of them that small?" Gary asked. I was grossed out. I wanted to leave.

"You know, as guy dancers grow-up, they need support," the sales lady pointed out. "I promise you, once you get used to them you'll wonder how you'd get by without them," she said smiling. I think she wanted to giggle.

"Guys, think of the dance belt as a bra for men," she said. "When girls grow up, they have to wear bras when they dance. Men have to wear dance belts." We felt like a couple of idiots. It's like she was speaking Dutch. We just looked at the garment lying on the sales desk with blank expressions.

"Not to worry, no one has worn these two belts before. It's our policy with dance belts. It's unsanitary to let guys try these on. Trust me, the smalls will fit you two just fine." She stuffed the dance belt back into the box.

"Is there anything thing else you guys need today?" said the lady.

"Ah, yes. No," I said. "We also need two pairs of black tights in our size," I added.

"Great, I'll get those from the back," she said happily. I pulled out my wallet to pay the bill.

"My Mom will pay you back tomorrow," Gary said.

"Ok," I said. Going down the elevator, we peeked in the bag and thought about wearing these things. Maybe they wouldn't be so bad. It was a quiet train ride home. The secret about dance belts now in our shopping bag. Why didn't anyone tell us about these torture undies? Well, I was about to find out.

I got home and headed for my room. Thank God, my little brother wasn't home. I stripped everything off. I opened the little box and emptied the measly contents on my bed. I picked up the garment and studied it for a minute. I really wasn't sure which was the front or back. I wanted to believe that the wide part was for my butt and the narrower section was for my giblets. Boy was I wrong.

"Holy shit," I said. After several miserable attempts to see if the wide part goes over the butt. I knew why no one told us about these things.

"Jesus, I can't believe this!" I turned the damn thing around so the wide side covered my man stuff and the small part slid up between my butt cheeks. Now, how to arrange the front equipment. Was I supposed to tuck my junk underneath? I tried that. After my voice raised a few octaves with things tucked under my crotch, I knew it wasn't right. I thought about how women adjust their bras. It all made sense. I loaded my equipment in the upward position, let the wide part of the garment snap back for a tight and snug hug to the waist. By this time, the irritation from the butt cheek strap had subsided. It wasn't so bad. Now for the tights.

Tights can look ridiculous on a guy, if they're not put on right. I remember wearing them for one of my Mom's recitals a few years back. I learned that you have to pull the tights up really high. If you don't, it looks like you pooped your pants or you're wearing a diaper. I did exactly that. I was on stage during a rehearsal and my Mom helped me pull up my tights. She grabbed the waist band and lifted me up. I slide down and the tights rode up my butt crack. She put a tight elastic strap around the waist to hold up the suckers, so they didn't slip down. The tights felt horrible, but I looked good.

So, the dance belt was on. I opened the plastic bag of black tights. I sat on my bed and began to weasel my feet into the footed tights. This was crazy. Do girls struggle this much putting tights on? I pulled and wrangled the waist part up past my belly button. Something was wrong.

"Damn it," I shouted. I put them on backwards. Off they came. I did a re-run of the process with the tights flipped around; Success! I pulled the stretchy material to conform with my body. I mean, really tight. I looked at the picture on the *Men's Tights* package. I secured the waist band with a canvass boy scout belt to hold them up. I looked in the door mirror and imagined how the gals in class would look at me. I thought, "Wow dude, you look hot!" I could hardly wait for the first rehearsal.

I hadn't heard from Gary since the train ride. I thought that he got everything figured out. He was smart. He knew what to do. I got my rehearsal stuff together and had my Dad drop me off at the Forest Bluff community theater. I had been here before but didn't remember were the dressing rooms were. I saw one of the girls from our dance school.

"Hi Lisa," I said.

"Hey Chucky," Lisa said. "I'm so glad you're dancing the Russian Dance this year. It's better with guys."

"Thanks," I said. "Where are the men's dressing rooms?" Lisa walked me to the right place. The rehearsal was to begin shortly. I changed into my rehearsal tights, with my amazing dance belt, white t-shirt and black ballet slippers. I checked myself out in the mirror and put on a headband as the finishing touch.

"Goddamn it," Gary said as he shoved the dressing room door in.

"Rehearsal starts in ten minutes!" I said. "Why are you so late?"

"I forgot my dance bag at the house and my mom had to go back to get my stuff," Gary said. He was panting and plopped down on one of the old stuffed chairs.

"Did you try everything on?" I asked. "Did the dance belt fit?

"Look, I know what to do," Gary shouted.

"Ok, just wondering. Sorry!" I said. There was a knock on the door.

"Rehearsal begins in five minutes," said the stage person. Another little knock came from the door.

"Is Gary in there, it's his mom." I held the door open for her.

"Hi Mrs. Deerfield," I said. She was out of breath too.

"Hey Gary, here's your dance bag," She said, tossing his dance bag on the floor next to his chair. Gary waved at his mother.

"Thanks Mom," he whined. I went to the stage were the Ballet Company Director was waiting. There were portable practice barres on stage. A warm-up was about to begin. All the dancers found a place at the barre. I got a spot in the middle of two girls about my age. I could follow them if I forgot the combinations. The pianist sat down and opened her music folder.

"Welcome everyone," said Mr. Viscount, the Director. "We will begin with a short warm-up before we start the rehearsal. I know this is the first day. I will forgive being tardy this day only! Going forward, you will not be excused. Now, stand in first position," he said. Gary was late. What the hell was he doing? The music started. I saw the downstage curtain being pushed to the wings. It was Gary, he snuck behind the Mr. Viscount, and ran to the nearest warm-up barre. He squeezed in between one of the old lady dancers and the girl who was playing the lead part of Clara. I kept screwing up the combinations. I couldn't believe my eyes. Gary had put his dance belt and tights on backwards. He wore an oversized t-shirt with a *'Screw U'* emblem on the front. He didn't secure his tights to his waist. Everyone could see his crotch getting lower with every exercise. He kept pulling up the slippery material. It looked like he was scratching his ass non-stop. While I felt bad for Gary, I was enjoying the entertainment. He could be such a butthead. The warm-up ended. Mr. Viscount rolled his eyes at Gary's buffoonish outfit.

"Ok, I want to see the corps dancers in Waltz of the Flowers," said Mr. Viscount. "Everyone else be ready to learn your choreography in thirty minutes." Gary took off to the dressing room. I followed.

"Holy shit," said Gary closing the dressing room door.

"I'll tell you how to put everything on right," I said.

"Jesus Christ. Fine. Show me," Gary said. The lesson on what goes where and how wasn't long. Gary swore the entire time. I couldn't stop laughing. Once he figured how to wear the dance belt and tights, he said,

"Hey, I look good man!" "Wait till those babes see me now." Humility didn't last long in Gary's world.

In spite of the dance belt malfunction spectacle, Gary continued to complain about wearing his dance belt. He would say that he prefers the freedom of wearing nothing at all. He talked about going commando or dance beltless one day. "*Not a good idea*, keep dreaming," I said.

Mr. Viscount finished working on our Russian Dance a couple of weeks later. He made the steps easy for Gary and me. He was happy and we felt good about the upcoming show. The costume designer and seamstress took our measurements for our Russian Cossack outfits. We were hyped.

We had performed three shows to sold out houses. The entire ballet company was excited about our last show and the cast party after the show.

"Break a leg," Mr. Viscount said as he passed by Gary and me backstage. Marvin Viscount was a very kind old man. He had been a professional ballet dancer in Canada. He was demanding but had a good deal of patience. We had done a good job in the show. Everyone high-fived us. Gary and I looked great in out Cossack costumes. Our pants were fitted well at the waist but loose in the crotch and legs to give us more room when we did our splits, sit kicks and coffee grinder tricks. We had moustaches gum spirited to our upper lips and Russian Cossack hats strapped to our heads.

"Last show kiddos, see you at the party," One of the older dancers said.

"Yeah, break a leg too," I said. I really liked some of these gals and so did Gary. He was excited about the cast party.

The third act of our Nutcracker began. The Land of The Sweets was our spotlight. The Mother Ginger dance with about twenty or so six-year olds was over. One of the Gumdrops tripped over Mother Ginger's skirt ruffles and sent the other half of kids rolling off the stage. The guy playing the role of Mother Ginger, on stilts, almost took a dive into the light trees on stage left. The audience went nuts and cheered. Gary and I were next.

"I did it," Gary said smiling.

"What?" I said. The music started. We leaped onto the stage. My focus was off. What did he mean by "I did it?" My thoughts scrambled. I knew this dance so well, my body jumped and kicked perfectly with the music. People applauded with each dancing trick. I looked over at Gary. He was not smiling. Something was up. I could see him reaching for his waist band in between steps. His Cossack pants were coming off, and so was his moustache. Ok, only twenty seconds left I thought. The music was getting louder. Time for the crowd pleaser, the coffee grinders! Gary and I dropped to our floor positions with heads raised to see the audience. We began whipping our right legs around like crazy. I snapped my head to check out Gary's costume. His Cossack pants were now down to his thighs. Thank God most of the crowd couldn't see what I saw and everyone backstage. His moustache hit the ground.

"Son of a bitch," I said out loud. No one could hear me. The music was blasting. I looked again. Gary wasn't wearing his dance belt. Not even dance trunks or underwear. I heard a loud "AWWWWW," from the crowd. A kid in the front row pointed at Gary. I tried not to notice the folly that was unzipping next to me. Our big ending was coming. I looked over at Gary and he was buck naked below the waist, his

Cossack pants raking the stage floor. He twisted so that the audience only saw his butt. He pulled up the pants and turned around to pose on one knee while I jumped into the air and pulled off solo air split. The dance ended. Gary, holding his pants up and I standing next to him stepped forward to bow. The crowd cheered. In spite of the Gary's commando glitch, we were a hit. Mr. Viscount stood back stage looking like a deer in headlights. As we exited though the wings, Mr. Viscount signaled us over. Gary turned pale.

"It's always a good to wear something underneath," Mr. Viscount said. Gary looked back and nodded his head.

"Yes Sir," Gary said. We headed to the dressing room.

"So, are you going to the cast party?" I asked.

"No way," said Gary. "After I stripped in front of the entire cast. Would you?" he said.

"You would have stripped in front of everyone sooner or later," I laughed. Gary took a few seconds to think about it.

"You're right," Gary said. "Now I don't have to introduce myself."

About the Author

KJ Lawlor has been a ballet teacher, choreographer and writer for over forty years. His passion for creative writing started in elementary school and continued through college and arts career. He has a B.A. in Communications from the University of South Florida and an A.S. is Physical Therapy from Polk State College. He holds the Teachers Advanced Grade VII certification of the Cecchetti Method of classical ballet. His interests include, aviation, sailing, carpentry, cooking, gardening, photography and music. He has three grown children. He lives in Florida with his wife Leena, two psychotic cats and a faithful dog.